The Christmas Quilt

Also by Jennifer Chiaverini in Large Print:

The Runaway Quilt
The Quilter's Apprentice
The Quilter's Legacy
The Master Quilter
The Sugar Camp Quilt

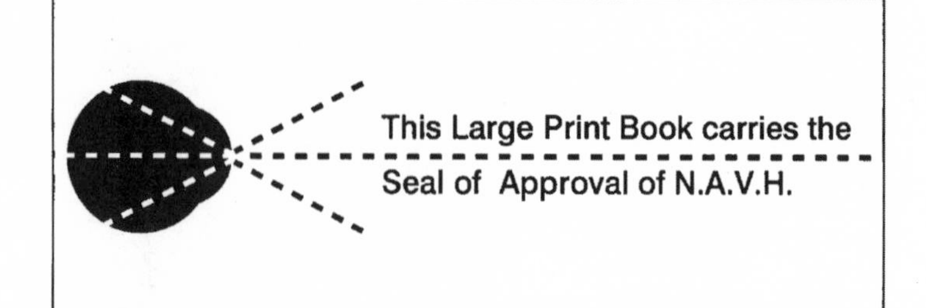

The Christmas Quilt

An Elm Creek Quilts Novel

Jennifer Chiaverini

Thorndike Press • Waterville, Maine

This book is a work of fiction. Names, characters, places, and incidents either are products of the author's imagination or are used fictitiously. Any resemblance to actual events or locales or persons, living or dead, is entirely coincidental.

Published in 2005 by arrangement with
Simon & Schuster, Inc.

Thorndike Press® Large Print Core.

The tree indicium is a trademark of Thorndike Press.

The text of this Large Print edition is unabridged.
Other aspects of the book may vary from the original edition.

Set in 16 pt. Plantin by Minnie B. Raven.

Printed in the United States on permanent paper.

Library of Congress Cataloging-in-Publication Data

Chiaverini, Jennifer.
The Christmas quilt : an Elm Creek quilts novel / by Jennifer Chiaverini.
p. cm. — (Thorndike Press large print core)
ISBN 0-7862-8073-5 (lg. print : hc : alk. paper)
1. Compson, Sylvia (Fictitious character) — Fiction. 2. Quiltmakers — Fiction. 3. Quilting — Fiction. 4. Quilts — Fiction. 5. Women — Fiction. 6. Large type books. 7. Christmas stories. 8. Domestic Fiction. I. Title. II. Thorndike Press large print core series.
PS3553.H473C48 2005b
813′.54—dc22 2005026552

To my grandparents,
Virginia and Edward Riechman

National Association for Visually Handicapped
serving the partially seeing

As the Founder/CEO of NAVH, the only national health agency solely devoted to those who, although not totally blind, have an eye disease which could lead to serious visual impairment, I am pleased to recognize Thorndike Press* as one of the leading publishers in the large print field.

Founded in 1954 in San Francisco to prepare large print textbooks for partially seeing children, NAVH became the pioneer and standard setting agency in the preparation of large type.

Today, those publishers who meet our standards carry the prestigious "Seal of Approval" indicating high quality large print. We are delighted that Thorndike Press is one of the publishers whose titles meet these standards. We are also pleased to recognize the significant contribution Thorndike Press is making in this important and growing field.

Lorraine H. Marchi, L.H.D.
Founder/CEO
NAVH

* Thorndike Press encompasses the following imprints: Thorndike, Wheeler, Walker and Large Print Press.

"I give you simply the joy and hope of the season."

— Gerda Bergstrom

Chapter One

Sylvia's childhood home was so full of memories it was a wonder there was any room for furniture. As the December days grew colder and the nights longer, the bygone years seemed to encroach ever more insistently into the present — vexing Sylvia day and night with their persistence. She imagined spirits of Christmases past crowding the halls, arguing over favorite chairs by the fire, looking about Elm Creek Manor, and shaking their heads in dismay over how she had let the place go. She would earn a small fortune if she could charge them rent, but regrettably, the spirits offered only longing whispers and mournful sighs. Nothing would appease them save an old-fashioned Bergstrom family Christmas, with all the trappings of the holiday, every beloved tradition fulfilled to the letter.

If Sylvia addressed the spirits — which she would not do, she was seventy-six but not quite ready to speak aloud to an empty room, thank you very much — she would warn them that they were bound to be disappointed. As much as Sylvia missed the Christmas joys of her youth, the Bergstroms were gone, every last one of them save Sylvia herself, and their traditions had passed on with them. Besides, Sylvia had a plan whose success depended upon this being the dullest, least festive, and most yawn-inducing Christmas in the history of Elm Creek Manor.

Her young friend Sarah McClure laughed off Sylvia's warnings of a dreary Christmas in their remote central Pennsylvania home. "Excitement is precisely what I'm trying to avoid," explained Sarah as she sewed three quilted stockings to hang before the fireplace in the library. "Christmas at my mother's house would be interesting, but for all the wrong reasons."

Exasperated, Sylvia strengthened her resolve to bring about reconciliation between Sarah and her mother. After all, Sarah had promised to try. A year and a half earlier, Sylvia had returned to Elm Creek Manor after a fifty-year absence, the sole heir to the Bergstrom estate upon the death of her estranged sister, Claudia. She had intended to sell it, but with Sarah's help, she made peace with her past and realized that she could never sell her beloved family home. The question remained, however, of how to restore life and happiness to the manor, which was much too large for one old woman living alone. Sarah had devised an ingenious solution, combining their love for quilting with their need for community by turning the Bergstrom estate into a summer retreat for quilters. As Sylvia and Sarah negotiated their business agreement, Sylvia, in repayment for all Sarah had done to help Sylvia reconcile with estranged loved ones, decided to add a clause that would encourage Sarah to mend fences in her own life.

"I don't know what kind of conflict stands between you and your mother," Sylvia had said, "but you must promise me you'll talk to her and do your best to resolve it. Don't be a stubborn fool like me and let grudges smolder and relationships die."

The unexpected request had clearly caught Sarah by surprise. "I don't think you know how difficult that will be."

"I don't pretend to know, but I can guess. I don't expect miracles. All I ask is that you learn from my mistakes and try."

Sarah had hesitated so long before making her reply that Sylvia had feared she would refuse and that their agreement to create Elm Creek Quilt Camp would fall through, but at last, Sarah agreed. Sylvia took her at her word and both women devoted themselves to the creation of Elm Creek Quilts. They worked so hard that first year to realize their vision that Sylvia could excuse Sarah's failure to make good on her promise. They were so busy, working fourteen-hour days or more with the help of Sarah's husband, Matt, and their talented staff of quilting teachers, that Sarah had no time to visit her mother and resolve their differences. But then camp ended for the summer, and still Sarah did little more than call her mother for a brief chat every other week. When she announced her intention to spend the holidays at Elm Creek Manor, Sylvia realized that Sarah would put off fulfilling her promise forever if she could get away with it. Since voiding their agreement was out of the question — Elm Creek Quilts had enriched Sylvia's life too much for her to throw it all away — she must see to it that her condition was fulfilled.

Sylvia figured there was no better time than Christmas to seek peace within a family, but Sarah could hardly reconcile with her mother from a hundred miles away. Somehow Sylvia would have to persuade Sarah that she would have a much merrier Christmas in her own childhood home, with a mother who loved her even if they did not always get along. Unfortunately, Sarah wasn't buying. Instead of seeking a happier holiday elsewhere, she had become determined to force a Merry Christmas upon Sylvia whether she wanted one or not.

If Sylvia had her way, she would observe Christmas as she had every season since abandoning her family estate for a modest home in Sewickley, Pennsylvania — church services in the morning, a Christmas concert on the radio after, perhaps dinner later at the home of a persistent friend who refused to heed Sylvia's firm assurances that she did not mind spending the holidays alone. It had always sufficed, and she had woken every December 26 relieved that she had made it through another Christmas without a fuss, without too many wistful reminiscences of holidays long past. But it had been much easier to ignore the whispers of memory from a distance. Now that she had returned home, she found herself longing to heed their call.

And if she didn't know better, she might suspect that Sarah knew how close she was to giving in, so often did she tempt her to abandon her plans for an unremarkable Christmas.

"Sylvia?" Sarah called from the hallway, moments before she appeared in the doorway to the kitchen where Sylvia was preparing a cup of tea. "Are you busy?"

Sylvia stirred honey into her tea. "I was just about to settle down with a good book."

"Then you have time to help me find the Christmas decorations."

"I already told you where to look." Sylvia carried her cup into the west sitting room, her favorite place to read or quilt. Sunlight streamed in through the windows shut tight against the cold. Through the bare branches of the stately elms outside, she glimpsed the bright red of the barn on the other side of Elm Creek, which was a slash of gray-blue cutting through the white crust of snow.

"You told me the decorations are in the attic. If you can't be more specific than that, it will be Easter before I find them."

Sylvia shrugged, lifted her book from where it lay facedown on her chair, and seated herself. "Perhaps you shouldn't bother then."

"Honestly, Sylvia," admonished Sarah. "It's the morning of Christmas Eve. If we don't decorate today, what's the point?"

"You're right. Why don't we forgo decorations this year? We'll have to take them down in a few days anyway. It hardly seems worth the effort."

Sarah stared at her in disbelief. "I half expected you to wrap that up with a 'Bah, humbug!' "

Sylvia slipped on her glasses, which hung from a fine silver chain around her neck. "I am neither a Scrooge nor a Grinch, thank you, but I have kept a quiet Christmas since before you were born. I warned you time and time again. If you wanted a more festive holiday, you and Matthew should have accepted your mother's invitation. I imagine her decorations are lovely."

Sarah frowned as she usually did whenever Sylvia brought up her mother. "My mother invited me, not Matt."

"Is that so? I assumed your husband was included implicitly. Husbands usually are for this sort of thing."

"You've never met my mother or you'd know better than to assume Matt's included unless she mentions him by name. She still hopes our wedding was a bad dream and she'll wake up one morning to find me engaged to my boyfriend from freshman year at Penn State."

Sylvia was certain Sarah was exaggerating. Matthew was a fine young man, and Sylvia could not imagine how Sarah's mother could possibly disapprove of their marriage as vehemently as Sarah claimed. "But what of your agreement to alternate visits between your side of the family and Matthew's? Since you spent last Christmas with his father, your mother was quite reasonable to expect you would visit her this year."

"We could have." Sarah sat down in the chair opposite Sylvia's. "Except that we wanted to have Christmas here, with you."

"Christmas is a time for family."

"You know you're like family to us. Elm Creek Manor is our home now. We couldn't bear to leave you in this big house all alone at Christmas time."

Sylvia feigned indifference and turned a page, although she had not read a word of it. "Don't lay the burden of your decision at my feet. I managed just fine last year."

"If we had known we were leaving you here by yourself, we would have stayed. You told us you were going to invite Agnes for Christmas dinner."

"My sister-in-law was out of town visiting one of her daughters."

"Yes, which you'd known since Thanksgiving but neglected to mention. Would you please put down that book and talk to me?"

Sylvia closed the book, marking her page with a finger, and peered at Sarah over the rims of her glasses. "Very well, young lady. I'm listening."

Sarah regarded her with fond exasperation. "You keep suggesting that if Matt and I wanted a festive Christmas, we should have gone somewhere else. I don't understand why we can't celebrate a Merry Christmas here, with you."

Privately, Sylvia acknowledged that Sarah had good reason to be puzzled. After all, they had so much worth celebrating: Sylvia's return to the family estate, the successful first year of Elm Creek Quilt Camp, new friends, and a future bright with possibilities. If anyone ought to be dancing about with a "Merry Christmas" on her lips, it should be Sylvia.

She should have known Sarah was too perceptive to be deceived by her simple ruse, but she wasn't quite ready to give up.

"I'm too old to make such a fuss," she said. "Christmas is for children."

She could tell from Sarah's expression that she had done little to dampen her young friend's enthusiasm. "Then long live childhood," Sarah declared. Sylvia sighed and opened her book again, but Sarah reached over and closed it. "You must have some Bergstrom family Christmas traditions you'd like to revive."

It was true; the Bergstroms had passed down many lovely Christmas traditions through the generations. The week before Christmas, the best cooks in the family would labor in the kitchen, turning out the most delicious treats — cookies, gingerbread, and strudel from her great-grandfather's sister's secret recipe. Delicious aromas of spices and baking once filled Elm Creek Manor at Christmastime, mingling with the scents of pine and holly and cinnamon. Every member of the family helped trim the stairways and mantels with freshly cut boughs, but only the most recently married couple was allowed to select the family Christmas tree. Before the south wing of the manor was constructed, the Christmas tree was displayed in the front parlor, but in later years it occupied the ballroom. They adorned the tree with the accumulated treasures of three generations — ceramic figurines from Germany, sparkling crystal teardrops from New York City, carved wooden angels with woolen hair from Italy. The children's favorite ornament was an eight-pointed glass star. Its red points with gold tips shone in the candlelight, casting flashes of brilliant color from floor to ceiling. On Christmas Eve, an adult would hide the star somewhere in the manor and send the children searching. The lucky child who found the star would win a prize, a small toy or bag of candy, and would be lifted high to place the star on the top of the tree. Twice Sylvia had found the star, but after her brother learned to walk, she always let him find it. Her sister had never found the star without the help of a kindly uncle whispering in her ear.

There was so much more, of course — memories crowded in of church services, music, stories, friends, and laughter. Yes, the Bergstroms had enjoyed many wonderful holiday traditions, but Sylvia did not think she could bear seeing them restored by well-meaning youngsters who could not truly understand their significance, especially if it meant that Sarah would postpone for yet another year a visit home for Christmas.

Undaunted by Sylvia's silence, Sarah persisted. "You can't be too old to sit back and enjoy Christmas decorations."

Sylvia sighed. There seemed little point

in preventing her. "Of course not."

Sarah took her hands. "Then keep me company in the attic while I look for the decorations. We have to put up a little tinsel and holly or Santa will think we've forgotten him."

Sarah insisted Sylvia precede her up the narrow, creaking attic steps — the better to break her fall should she stumble, Sylvia supposed. She shivered in the chilly darkness as Sarah stepped around her toward the center of the space. With a tug on the pull cord, pale light from the single, bare bulb spilled down, illuminating a circle of floorboards. Stacks of trunks, cartons, and old furniture cast deep shadows in the corners beyond the reach of the light.

To Sylvia's right lay the older west wing of the manor, the original home of the Bergstrom family, built in the middle of the nineteenth century by the first Bergstroms to immigrate to America from Germany. Directly before her stretched the south wing, added when her father was a boy. In the attic, the seams joining the original house and the addition were more evident than on the first three stories, the color of the walls subtly different, the floor not quite even. Little visible evidence betrayed that fact, as the belongings of four generations of her family covered nearly every square foot of floor space.

Sarah surveyed the attic with satisfaction, in all likelihood congratulating herself for finally persuading Sylvia upstairs. "Well? Where should we begin?"

Sylvia hadn't the faintest idea. Since returning from her self-imposed exile, she had visited the attic as infrequently as possible. She had not sought out the boxes of Christmas trimmings in more than fifty years.

"Over this way, I suppose," Sylvia told Sarah, gesturing toward what she guessed was the general location of two trunks, one green and one blue, and one sturdy carton. At first she stood aside and let Sarah do the work, but soon she began to feel foolish and impatient standing idle, so she joined in the search.

"I think I've found something," called Sarah from the other side of the trap door. Sylvia watched as she dragged a long rectangular box into the open, her wavy brown hair falling onto her face. The box, embellished with a forest of green pines, announced in red ink, "Festive Christmas Tree." Smaller black print identified the product as, "Evergleam. Made in Manitowoc, Wisconsin, U.S.A."

"I've never seen that before," said Sylvia, dusting off her hands and coming closer for a better look. Sarah opened one end of the box, reached inside, and with some effort pulled out a handful of what appeared to be wood shavings as shiny as tinfoil.

"It's one of those aluminum Christmas trees," said Sarah, delighted. "My grandmother used to have one."

"Mine didn't," said Sylvia dryly, imagining her father's mother recoiling in horror at the very thought. "This must be one of Claudia's more recent contributions to the estate. It reflects her taste."

"Oh, don't be so hard on her. These were the height of fashion once." Sylvia tugged until more of the atrocious foil tree emerged from the box.

"Hmph. If you say so."

"Would you mind if I set it up in my room?"

"If your husband can bear it, you may do whatever you like." Sylvia quickly amended, "As long as you promise to keep it out of my sight."

"I wonder if it came with one of those rotating colored floodlights like my grandmother had." Sarah disappeared behind an old wardrobe, her voice momentarily replaced by the sound of boxes scuffing across the floor. "Wait a minute. Sylvia? What color did you say those trunks were?"

"One was blue and one green." Sylvia picked her way through the clutter to join Sarah, who was removing a paint-spattered drop cloth from the top of a dusty forest green trunk with brass fastenings. "My word. You found it."

"Here's the other one," said Sarah, beaming up at Sylvia in triumph, resting her hand on a blue trunk. "The carton must be nearby."

"One would think so. There," said Sylvia. She could not help but be pleased to see them. Claudia had sold off so many things in Sylvia's absence that she had prepared herself for the possibility that they would not have found the trunks in the attic. The Bergstroms' old ornaments and trims probably had no more than sentimental value, but Sylvia would not have put it past Claudia to part with them for pocket change.

She tried to talk Sarah into waiting until her husband came home to carry the trunks and carton downstairs, but Sarah insisted upon doing it herself. It took four trips, but Sarah managed with Sylvia doing little more to help than barking anxious directions when her young friend seemed likely to tumble down the stairwell. After the last was settled three floors down in the foyer, Sarah barely paused to catch her breath before throwing back the lid of the blue trunk. Sylvia looked on warily, wondering if her sister had replaced their family heirlooms with thin aluminum varieties, but she relaxed at the sight of the green-and-red tartan tablecloth and a garland of gold beads. One familiar treasure after another — a wooden nativity set her grandfather had carved, eight personalized Christmas stockings, a china angel blowing a brass horn, the family Christmas tree ornaments — emerged from the trunk looking exactly as they had when she last packed them away, as if they had not been disturbed in more than fifty years.

Was it possible that her sister had never opened the boxes in all that time?

As Sarah turned to the second trunk, Sylvia sat down on the floor beside her, marveling over each item as Sarah passed them to her. Her brother's nutcracker, dressed in the bright red coat of a soldier, a sword in his fist. The wooden music box shaped like a sleigh full of toys that played "God Rest Ye Merry, Gentlemen" when the key was wound. The paper angels she and Claudia had made in Sunday school. A wreath made of pinecones she and her mother had gathered in the forest along Elm Creek. The memory of a snowy afternoon flooded her — the sound of her mother's laughter, the crisp winter air nipping her cheeks — and she clutched the wreath so tightly that brittle pieces broke off in her fingers.

She gasped and set the wreath on the floor. Sarah glanced over her shoulder, her expression darkening with concern. "Are you all right?"

"I'm fine." Sylvia shifted on the floor so that Sarah would think discomfort rather than grief had provoked her. She forced a smile. "Well. You should have plenty of decorations to work with, don't you agree?"

"Enough for the entire manor, but before I get started, I want to see what's in those other two boxes."

"Two?" Sylvia checked, and sure enough, two cartons sat on the marble floor just beyond the trunks. "Goodness. If I had paid more attention I could have saved you that last trip upstairs. I said two trunks and one carton, remember?"

Sarah shrugged, returning her attention

to the contents of the green trunk. "I know, but I peeked inside and saw some Christmasy colors, so I brought them both down. Maybe Claudia added to the collection while you were away."

Judging by the metal tree her sister had acquired, Sylvia certainly hoped not. She went to the nearest carton and pulled open the flaps. There she discovered more familiar decorations — candlesticks, china teacups and saucers encircled with pictures of holly leaves and berries, the jolly Santa Claus cookie jar Great-Aunt Lucinda kept filled with lebkuchen, anisplätzchen, and zimtsterne from St. Nicholas Day through the Feast of the Three Kings. She sorted through the carton, each discovery rekindling a long-neglected memory until it was almost too much for her to continue. When she finished, she scanned the items Sarah had laid out on the floor as she emptied the trunks. Nothing seemed to be missing except for the ruby star for the top of the tree, which had been lost long ago — but what, then, filled the last box?

"Perhaps you should open that one," said Sylvia, less than enthusiastic at the prospect of discovering more of her sister's garish purchases.

Sarah dusted off her hands and opened the last carton. "Good news. I told you I didn't waste a trip to the attic. It's more Christmas stuff."

"What's the bad news?"

"There is no bad news. Come and see for yourself." Sarah grinned over her shoulder at Sylvia, amused by her wariness. "I'm sure you'll like it. It's fabric, not foil."

A memory tickled the back of Sylvia's mind, but as soon as she peered inside the box, the memory struck with the full force of a blow. "Oh, my goodness."

"What is it?"

Sylvia sank to her knees beside the box, overwhelmed by the sensation of discovery and loss. She had never forgotten the Christmas Quilt, nor had she ever expected to see it again. Begun by her Great-Aunt Lucinda when Sylvia was very young, the unfinished quilt had been taken up and worked upon by a succession of Bergstrom women — among them, Sylvia herself. From what she could see of the folded bundle of patchwork and appliqué, not a single stitch had been added since she last worked upon it. And yet every intricate Feathered Star block, every graceful appliquéd cluster of holly leaves and berries had been tucked away as neatly as if a conscientious quiltmaker had had every intention of completing her masterpiece. Even the scraps of fabric had been sorted according to color — greens here, reds there, golds and creams in their own separate piles. The Christmas Quilt had been abandoned, but it had not been discarded.

Had Claudia intended to finish it herself one day, only to find that it evoked too many painful memories? She had borne no children, so she could not have meant to leave it for a member of the next generation to finish, as their great-aunt and mother had, each in her turn. She certainly could not have been saving the quilt for Sylvia's homecoming.

How many Christmases had her sister spent in Elm Creek Manor, alone and longing, haunted by memories of more joyful times long past?

"Sylvia?" Sarah placed a hand upon Sylvia's, concerned. "What's wrong?"

"Oh, you know how it is with me every time you insist upon poking around in this old place." Sylvia patted Sarah's hand and sighed. For Sarah it was great fun, a trip back in time into the history of Elm Creek Manor. For Sylvia it was something else entirely. "Whenever we stumble upon some old artifact from Bergstrom family history, I'm reminded of how I failed my ancestors by walking out, by allowing everything they spent their lives building to fall apart."

"You left, but you also returned," Sarah reminded her, as she always did. "Elm Creek Manor still stands, and you brought life back to it. Your family would be proud."

"Astonished, yes. Proud?" Sylvia shook her head. "I'm not so certain."

Sarah smiled, understanding her perfectly. "Granted, they probably never imagined the manor as a quilters' retreat, but everything you've told me about them suggests they valued art and education and community. Isn't that what Elm Creek Quilts stands for?"

Sylvia considered. "Perhaps you're right."

"I know I'm right." Sarah reached into the box and took out a folded bundle of patchwork. "You never mentioned a long-lost Christmas quilt." She unfolded the fabric and discovered that instead of a finished quilt top, she held only a strip of Log Cabin blocks sewn together and wrapped around a small stack of additional blocks. "Oh. It's a UFO."

"It is indeed an Unfinished Fabric Object, and destined to remain so." Sylvia removed the next carefully folded bundle, and felt a twist of painful longing in her heart upon recognizing her mother's handiwork, the perfect appliqué stitches that were her trademark. "My great-aunt Lucinda began this quilt before I was born. It became something of a family joke. Every November she would take it from her sewing basket and declare that this year she would finish it in time for Christmas morning. Of course she never did, and once the holidays passed, she would lose interest in it and pack it away. I understand her point; who thinks about Christmas projects in April? But without fail, when Thanksgiving rolled around, she'd get in a Christmas mood again and pick up where she left off." Sylvia nodded to a thin stack of green-and-red Feathered Star blocks as Sarah removed them from the box. "She made those. Her original design called for twenty, if I remember correctly, but I don't believe she ever made more than six."

"And then she switched to Variable Stars?" guessed Sarah, glancing inside the box at what remained.

"Good heavens, no. Lucinda wouldn't have resorted to something so simple after devoting years to these Feathered Stars." With a sniff, Sylvia dismissed the blocks remaining within the carton. "Claudia pieced the Variable Stars when she took it upon herself to finish the quilt. Before my sister got her hands on it, my mother appliquéd these holly wreaths." Sylvia remembered all too well the day her mother had set the quilt aside, and why. Years later, Sylvia tried to finish what the other women of her family had begun, thinking, wrongly, that her Log Cabin blocks would pull the disparate pieces together. "I'm afraid what you see here amounts to nothing more than good intentions gone awry. Or rather, gone nowhere."

Sarah's glance took in the different sections of the quilt. "We could finish it."

Sylvia snapped out a laugh. "I don't think so."

"Why not? We've finished other quilts together. My sampler, the memorial quilt Claudia and Agnes made from your husband's clothes —"

"That's different. Those quilts were begun in special circumstances."

"And this quilt wasn't?"

"Well —" Sylvia fumbled for an excuse. "We won't have time to quilt, dear. Have you forgotten? We have Christmas decorations to put up."

Sarah regarded her skeptically. "Not twenty minutes ago you insisted that there was no reason to decorate for Christmas, and now it's more important than working on this quilt?"

"I suppose I've come around to your way of thinking. I believe you underestimate how long it takes to decorate such a large house. Then there's Christmas dinner to make, and church services in the morning, and I have gifts for you and Matthew. By the time we get to the quilt, you'll find that Christmas is over and you won't feel like working on it anymore, just like my great-aunt Lucinda."

"All the more reason to work on it now, while I'm full of Christmas cheer."

Sylvia indicated the trunks and cartons and decorations Sarah had spread out on the floor. "So you intend to leave the foyer in this state, after dragging those heavy trunks down from the attic?"

Sarah surveyed the mess guiltily. "I suppose I should tidy up first."

"I can take care of it myself if you need the time to pack —"

"Sylvia, for the last time, I'm not going to my mother's for Christmas."

"Well, don't expect me to help you with

that quilt when we both know you ought to be in a car on your way to Uniontown," said Sylvia, finally out of patience. She knew that the moment Sarah decided to finish that quilt, she had dealt Sylvia's plan a staggering blow. And time was running out.

Sarah returned the pieces of the Christmas Quilt to the box, but the affectionate pat she gave Great-Aunt Lucinda's Feathered Stars told Sylvia they wouldn't remain set aside for long. As Sylvia suspected she would, the young woman also declared that since the decorations were already down from the attic and out of the boxes and trunks, it made more sense to put them up than to put them away. Sylvia decided to leave her to it, so she returned to the west sitting room and her book, and the cup of tea that had long since grown cold.

Exasperated, she went to the kitchen to put the kettle on, shaking her head at Sarah's irrepressibility. Now Sarah had a decorating plan and a quilt to keep her in the manor. Once that young lady caught hold of a fanciful idea, she would not let go until it sent her soaring off into the clouds as if it were the tail of some enormous kite.

She always managed to latch on to some grand scheme. Creating a quilt camp, for example. Or convincing a bitter old woman to take a second chance on life.

Then again, compared to what Sarah had already accomplished, finishing a quilt that had daunted several more experienced quilters might prove to be a simple matter.

The kettle whistled and sent up a thin jet of white steam. Sylvia poured and waited for the tea to steep, lost in thought. From down the hall, faint music drifted to her ear. Curious, she quickly stirred honey into her cup and carried it back to the foyer. Sarah had accomplished little in the way of tidying up, but she had hung wreaths on the two tall double doors of the manor's front entrance and had strung garlands along the grand oak staircase. In the corner she had plugged in her CD player, which was responsible for the strains of "White Christmas" that had beckoned Sylvia from the kitchen.

"Things are shaping up nicely here," remarked Sylvia, looking about the foyer.

Sarah glanced up from sorting through a box of ornaments and smiled. "Later I'll call Matt on his cell phone and ask him to bring home a Christmas tree from the lot at the mall."

"Nonsense. I won't have him pay ten dollars a foot for a tree when we have plenty to choose from right here on the estate. Besides, you're supposed to bring in the tree together."

"He *is* a landscape architect. If he can tend an orchard I'm sure he can pick out a Christmas tree."

"I'm not questioning his qualifications, but in my family we always . . ."

When she did not continue, Sarah prompted, "You always what?"

"We always . . . saved our money for more important things and cut down a tree from our own woods. But you and Matthew may do whatever you like."

"So you won't mind having a Christmas tree?"

"Not as long as you sweep up the fallen needles."

"It's a deal." Sarah gave the ornaments one last admiring look, rose, and made a show of checking her watch. "Ten o'clock. I think it's time for a quilting break."

"But you just started."

In reply, Sarah simply picked up the box holding the pieces of the Christmas Quilt.

Clutching her teacup, Sylvia trailed after Sarah, down the hall and through the kitchen to the west sitting room. Frowning,

Sylvia sat down in her favorite chair by the window and picked up her book, studiously ignoring Sarah as she spread out the various sections of the incomplete quilt on the sofa and the rug. The younger woman studied the Bergstrom women's handiwork for several minutes in silence before she spoke. "I think we have enough for a complete quilt right here."

Sylvia closed her book. "Don't be ridiculous. It couldn't possibly be that easy or one of us would have done it years ago."

Sarah peered closely at the patchwork and appliqué, considering. "Maybe it took an objective outsider to see the possibilities."

"Young lady, I've been quilting much longer than you have. A person can stitch together any two pieces of fabric in any haphazard way they choose and call it a quilt, but unless you've lowered your standards, I expect you to strive for something that also pleases the eye. That simply isn't possible with what you see here. You don't have enough of any one of the blocks for a complete quilt, and yet you don't have enough variety for an attractive sampler."

"No, look," said Sarah, rearranging two of the appliquéd holly plumes so that they flanked one of Claudia's Variable Stars.

"This could be the center of the quilt. We could set the Feathered Star blocks around them, kind of like a rectangle with the other Variable Stars in the corners. The Feathered Star blocks will be the focus of the quilt, which is perfect because they're so beautifully made."

"Indeed they are," said Sylvia, proud of her great-aunt. "You could always leave out my sister's Variable Stars rather than risk ruining the quilt. Accuracy was never her strong suit. Some of those blocks don't look to be true squares."

"I wouldn't dream of leaving Claudia out of a family quilt. I'm sure her blocks are accurate enough."

Sylvia was far less certain, and she could cite a wealth of evidence to support her assessment of Claudia's piecing skills, but she did not feel like arguing — and, she reminded herself, it did not matter to her whether this quilt would ever be finished. So she settled back down with her book and her now lukewarm cup of tea, but after reading a few lines, Sarah's shuffling of blocks and patches drew her attention. She had arranged Great-Aunt Lucinda's six Feathered Star blocks in an elongated ring — two on one side, two on the other, and one on each end. Sylvia had to admit the placement would complement the exquisite blocks. Lucinda had pieced all of her quilts by hand and was as precise and exacting in her sewing as she was generous and forgiving in every other aspect of her life. She was Sylvia's grandfather's youngest sister, the baby of their family, and perhaps that was why the others teased her so affectionately about her repeated failures to complete the Christmas Quilt. In Sylvia's earliest childhood memories, Lucinda always appeared as a patient and reassuring figure, calm and wise — and old, although in hindsight Sylvia realized she was probably not yet fifty when she set aside the Christmas Quilt for the last time.

In fair weather Lucinda enjoyed sewing on the front veranda, but the approach of autumn beckoned her inside to the front parlor, which looked out upon the veranda and the broad, sweeping lawn that separated the house from the forest. Sylvia, who had not yet learned to quilt, often watched her aunt drawing templates for a new quilt with a freshly sharpened pencil, carefully tracing their shapes on the wrong side of brightly colored fabrics, and cutting out the pieces with brisk snips of her shears. Sylvia hung on to the arm of her chair as she sewed, watching and pestering

Lucinda with questions as she stitched four small, cream-colored triangles to a larger octagon cut from cheerful red fabric. Eager to help, she paired green triangles with white so they would be ready for her great-aunt's needle. Sylvia admired the intricate blocks, which she thought resembled green snowflakes with red tips. As the fifth Feathered Star took shape, Sylvia begged Lucinda to teach her how to make one. "I will teach you to quilt someday," promised Lucinda, "but this pattern is too difficult for a little girl's first project. Let's make a Log Cabin quilt instead."

"When?" persisted Sylvia. "When can we start?"

With a nod, Lucinda indicated the Feathered Star pieces spread on her lap. "After I finish my Christmas Quilt, we will begin yours."

Thrilled, Sylvia raced off to tell her older sister the news, secretly pleased when Claudia tossed her brown curls and declared that she was too busy helping Mother to quilt with Great-Aunt Lucinda, a sure sign that she was sick with jealousy. Then Claudia added, "Everyone says she'll never finish that quilt, anyway."

"She will so," snapped Sylvia and marched back to the parlor to help. She had heard the teasing remarks, too, but they had never been a cause for worry until now.

To Sylvia's relief, her great-aunt kept up an industrious pace and showed no signs of abandoning her quilt. As Christmas approached, Sylvia forgot her worries in the excitement of the season. She and Claudia were both chosen to participate in the Christmas pageant at school — Claudia as an angel, Sylvia as a lamb. Between rehearsing for the pageant and practicing with the children's choir at church, helping Grandma with the baking and secretly working on Christmas gifts for the family, Sylvia had little time to spare for observing the Christmas Quilt. Still, Great-Aunt Lucinda made good progress despite Sylvia's absence from her side every hour of the day. Although she did take time away from her sewing to bake Christmas cookies, she always returned to her Feathered Stars by evening. Sylvia's quilting lessons would surely begin before the end of winter.

The approach of Christmas brought visitors to Elm Creek Manor, friends and relatives from near and far. Best of all was the day Sylvia's beloved second cousin Elizabeth returned, accompanied by her parents. For the past five summers, she had come to Elm Creek Manor to help care for the children and, as she said, "enjoy the fresh country air." Sometimes she went riding with a boy her age from a neighboring farm, but except for those annoying interruptions, she was Sylvia's nearly constant companion, favorite playmate, and most trusted confidante. Sylvia could not help but adore her; Elizabeth was kind and funny and smart and beautiful — all the things Sylvia hoped to be when she grew up.

Elizabeth was barely in the door before Sylvia was tugging off her coat and seizing her hand to lead her off on some secret adventure. Elizabeth laughingly obliged, shaking snow from her hair and handing off her mittens to her mother, but she seemed distracted and quiet. When Sylvia asked her what was wrong, Elizabeth looked surprised. "Nothing," she said. "Everything is wonderful." Then she tickled Sylvia and acted like the old Elizabeth so convincingly that Sylvia decided to believe her.

Great-Aunt Lucinda finished her fifth Feathered Star block on the morning of Christmas Eve. "Only fifteen more to go," she told Sylvia at breakfast, and Sylvia's heart sank in despair. So many blocks stood between her and her lessons! But she brightened up when Elizabeth came to the table, breathless and apologizing for her tardiness, her long golden hair tied back in a grosgrain ribbon the color of the winter sky. Sylvia had a ribbon almost the exact same hue, and if Elizabeth helped Sylvia fix her hair the same way, they could be twins — except that Sylvia's hair was dark brown.

After breakfast, Uncle William and his wife went out to find the Christmas tree, sent on their way with teasing and laughter and strange remarks from the other grown-ups that Sylvia suspected she only partially understood. The couple had been married less than a year, and Sylvia overheard her grandmother say that it would be a very bad sign if they were gone more than two hours.

"It will be a far worse sign if they're back within thirty minutes," Sylvia's father replied. The uncles grinned and the aunts nodded thoughtfully. Sylvia looked around at the faces of her family, puzzled. If they found a perfect tree right away and brought it home as quickly as they could cut it down, what could be wrong with that? They could begin trimming the tree sooner, and Sylvia couldn't wait. The previous day, she and Claudia had helped Elizabeth and their grandmother unpack the two trunks of Christmas ornaments. They'd had a wonderful time admiring their favorite pieces, singing carols, and munching on Great-Aunt Lucinda's lebkuchen still warm from the oven — until a cousin appeared in the doorway and called Elizabeth away to meet a visitor. Elizabeth rushed off with barely a word of good-bye, but Sylvia had not minded until dinnertime, when she discovered that the visitor was that man Elizabeth used to go riding with in the summers, and that he had taken the seat beside Elizabeth Sylvia usually reserved for herself. She scowled at him from across the table, but he merely smiled pleasantly back, so he was obviously not smart enough to understand when someone was angry with him.

The newlyweds returned with a tree not quite two hours after they had departed. "That's just about right," Sylvia's grandmother told Lucinda as they trailed after the rest of the family to the ballroom, where the tree would be raised. Her voice was so soft that Sylvia knew she was not meant to overhear. "Any sooner and I'd worry that she wouldn't be strong enough for him."

"William can be stubborn," said Lucinda. "I suspect he gave in quickly rather than displease his lovely bride. That contrary behavior can't possibly last. We'll see how long it takes them next year, and whether they're still speaking when they return home."

"*If* they'll be eligible to choose the tree next year," said Grandmother archly. "I suspect they may not be allowed a second turn."

The women exchanged knowing smiles and disappeared into the ballroom. Sylvia stopped in the foyer, frowning as she mulled over their words. Why shouldn't Uncle William and his wife be allowed to pick the tree again? There wasn't anything wrong with the one they had chosen. Was Great-Aunt Lucinda jealous because she had never been allowed a turn? Sylvia searched her memory but could not recall any other time when her great-aunt had seemed envious. Well, if Great-Aunt Lucinda wanted to pick the Christmas tree, she would just have to get married. That's what the rules said, and Sylvia strongly disapproved of anyone — even Great-Aunt Lucinda — thinking she could simply toss out the family's rules when it suited.

Noise and laughter beckoned her from her worries, and she hurried into the ballroom rather than miss all the fun. As young and old adorned the branches of Uncle William's tree with their favorite ornaments, Great-Aunt Lucinda told them stories of long-ago Christmases when her mother, Sylvia's great-grandmother Anneke, was a little girl in Germany. Sylvia was surprised to learn that her great-grandmother had not been allowed to help decorate the Christmas tree. "None of the children were," explained Great-Aunt Lucinda. "The adults of the family decorated the tree while the children waited in another room. On Christmas Eve, her mother would ring a bell and all the children would come running in to admire the tree and eat delicious treats — cookies and nuts and fruits. My mother and the other girls and boys would search the branches of the tree, and whoever found the lucky pickle would win a prize."

"A pickle?" said Sylvia. "How did a pickle get in their tree?"

"Not a real pickle, dear. A glass pickle, an ornament. Her mother or father would hide it there before the children came in." Great-Aunt Lucinda paused thoughtfully. "I suppose that's where our tradition of hiding the Christmas star came from."

"Did Santa bring her presents?" asked Claudia.

"Not on Christmas," said Lucinda. "Of course you know that Santa Claus is really St. Nicholas, and that we celebrate his day on December 6. On the night before, Great-Grandmother Anneke and her brothers and sisters would each leave a shoe by the fireplace, just as you children hang stockings. If they had been good children all year, when they woke in the morning, they would find their shoes filled with candy, nuts, and fruit. If they had been naughty, they might find coal or twigs. One year, my uncle found an onion. I always wondered what he had done to deserve that."

"But we get St. Nicholas Day and Christmas," said Sylvia. It didn't seem fair that her great-grandmother had not.

"You are very lucky children," Great-Aunt Lucinda pronounced. "You're fortunate in another regard, too. In your great-grandmother's day, St. Nicholas traveled with a helper named Knecht Ruprecht. He carried St. Nicholas's bag of treats for him, and it was he who went up and down the chimneys filling the children's shoes. But he also carried a sack and a stick. He used the stick to beat the naughty little children, and if a child was very, very bad, Knecht Ruprecht would stuff him in the sack and carry him off, never to see his family again."

Sylvia shivered.

"Aunt Lucinda, you're frightening the children," said Sylvia's mother.

"Why should these children be scared?" protested Great-Aunt Lucinda. She looked around the circle of worried young faces, brow furrowing in concern. "None of you children were naughty this year, were you?"

The children shook their heads fervently, but as they did, Sylvia thought of the times she had argued with her sister, disobeyed her parents, and taken cookies from Great-Aunt Lucinda's cookie jar without permission. She hoped Knecht Ruprecht had stayed behind in Germany with the pickle trees.

"Perhaps a less alarming story, Aunt Lucinda?" prompted Sylvia's mother.

Great-Aunt Lucinda played along. "Did I ever tell you children about the Bergstroms' first Christmas in America?"

They shook their heads.

"I've been remiss, then." She composed her thoughts for a moment. "Your great-grandfather, Hans, arrived in America several years before Anneke and Gerda — Hans's sister — but their first Christmas together wasn't until 1856. The stone house that we now know as the west wing of the manor wouldn't be built for another two years, so for a time they lived in a log cabin on the land they called Elm Creek Farm. Hans and Anneke were newlyweds, and Anneke was determined to make their first Christmas one to remember, as grand an affair as she would have put on had she been a hausfrau in Berlin, the city of her birth.

"As you can imagine, this was not easily done. The Bergstroms were recent immigrants living in a small cabin in the middle of rural Pennsylvania. They had the land, some livestock, and the stores of their first harvest, but none of the comforts we enjoy today. Anneke wanted a goose for Christmas dinner, but there were none to be had. She wanted to give her new husband a gift that befitted her love for him, but the shops in town had nothing suitable that she could afford."

"And no pickles for the trees?" asked Sylvia.

"Not a single pickle," said Great-Aunt Lucinda. "On Christmas Eve, Gerda discovered Anneke digging through the steamer trunk she had brought over from Germany. Anneke confessed that she was searching for a Christmas gift for Hans, but she had found nothing worthy of him. 'What will he think of me,' lamented Anneke, 'if I have no gift for him on Christmas morning?'

" 'Do you think my brother loves you for the things you give him?' asked Gerda. 'Give him the gift of your heart and your company, and he will want nothing more.'

" 'But I've already given him those,' said Anneke.

" 'Then he already has his heart's desire.'

"Anneke seemed comforted by this, but not completely satisfied. So late that night, after everyone else had gone to bed, she wrote Hans a letter telling him how much she loved him and how much she looked forward to their future together. On Christmas morning, she gave him the letter. He read it in silence, and when he finished, he hugged her and told her it was the greatest present he had ever received."

"Did Hans get her anything?" asked Claudia.

Great-Aunt Lucinda considered. "I suppose he did, but the story doesn't say. I do know what Gerda gave Hans and Anneke, though. She had traded with a neighbor for two shiny, red, perfect apples, and as she gave one to her brother and one to her sister-in-law, she said, 'I give you simply the joy and hope of the season.' "

At this the grown-ups nodded and murmured in approval, but Sylvia frowned. "She gave them apples?"

"They were more than just apples," said Great-Aunt Lucinda. "Think of the sweetness of the fruit and the promise in the seeds. In that simple gift, Gerda was expressing how joyful her life was with Hans and Anneke, and how full of blessings their future would be."

Claudia looked dubious. "They were just apples."

"They were not just apples," said Great-Aunt Lucinda firmly. "They were expressions of her love and hopes, simply and eloquently presented. Don't you see? You can give someone all the riches of the world, but it is an empty gesture if you withhold the gift of yourself."

"I think that's beyond their understanding," said Uncle William with a grin. "They're awfully young for such philosophizing."

"Perhaps." Great-Aunt Lucinda looked around the circle of young, curious faces until her gaze settled on Sylvia. "If they don't understand today, someday they will."

Sylvia longed to show Lucinda that she understood, but she was not sure that she did. An apple didn't seem like much of a present to her, but maybe back in the olden days, apples were considered wonderful gifts. Maybe, she thought suddenly, Hans and Anneke had planted the seeds of the apples Gerda had given them. Maybe those very seeds grew into the orchard their family tended and enjoyed today. If that were true, Gerda had indeed given Hans and Anneke the joy and hope of the season — and continued to give it, with every harvest, to their descendants.

When the tree decorating was almost finished, Grandmother entrusted Elizabeth, her namesake, with the task of hiding the glass star somewhere in the manor. Sylvia hoped Elizabeth would give her a secret clue to help her find the star before the others, but a few minutes later, Elizabeth slipped back into the room, whispered close to her grandmother's ear, and smiled equally warmly at all her young cousins. If anything, her gaze lingered longest on her friend, that man from the neighboring farm, who had reappeared while the family was setting the tree in its stand and showed no sign of leaving anytime soon. With dismay, Sylvia realized that she would probably lose her favorite seat at the dinner table two nights in a row.

Lost in this new troublesome concern, she did not hear her grandmother send out the children to search for the star. "Sylvia," she heard her mother call. "Aren't you going to help find the star this year?"

Sylvia raced for the ballroom door, but Claudia and the cousins had made a good head start. She could only watch from a distance as they sped off in all directions, intent upon reaching the manor's best hiding places first. She ran for the front parlor, where Claudia had found the star the previous year, only to discover that a cousin had already claimed that room. She ran upstairs to the library, but two other cousins were already searching there. In every room it was the same: Claudia and the cousins raced about, laughing and shrieking and tearing the house apart in their quest for the star, leaving Sylvia with no choice but to dart out of the way.

Miserable, Sylvia went to the bedroom she and Claudia shared, knowing it was the one place no one would bother her. All of the fun had gone out of the game, but she would be disgraced if she returned to the ballroom before the star was found. Squeezing her eyes shut to hold back tears, she flung herself upon the bed — and gasped when her head struck something hard beneath the pillow. In a moment she was sitting upright on the bed, the star in her lap, its eight red-and-gold points glistening faintly in the dim light.

The star, beneath her own pillow. Elizabeth had left it where no one else would think to look. She had left it especially for Sylvia, her favorite.

Bursting with pride and gratitude, Sylvia climbed down from the bed and hurried downstairs, clutching the precious glass star to her chest. "I found it," she called out as she ran. "I found it!" She burst into the ballroom, breathless. "I found the star!"

The adults crowded around her, offering her hugs and congratulations. Someone called out to the other children that the game was over. In the distance, Sylvia heard their answering cries of dismay.

"Where did you find it?" one of the uncles asked.

Sylvia could not bring herself to tell him.

"Upstairs," she said, and her eyes met Elizabeth's. Her cousin smiled at her, bright-eyed and mischievous, and raised a single finger to her lips. Sylvia, suddenly warmed by happiness, smiled until she laughed out loud.

The prize her grandmother awarded her was a small tin filled with red-and-white striped peppermint candy. At her mother's prompting, Sylvia offered each of the other children a piece, and her joy in the secret she and Elizabeth shared made it hardly matter at all that the tin was returned to her half empty.

All the while, Sylvia clung to the Christmas star. Suddenly, strong arms swept her up. "It's time, little miss," her father said, lifting her high above his head beside the tree. "Reach for the highest branch. You can do it."

Sylvia stretched out her arms and fit the star upon a strong bough that pointed straight up to the ceiling. Everyone applauded as her father lowered her to the ground. As the aunts lit the candles upon the tree, Sylvia stepped back so she could take in the whole of it, from the quilted skirt draped around the trunk to the star she had placed so perfectly upon the very top.

"It's beautiful," said Elizabeth. Her

friend smiled and placed an arm around her shoulders, and she leaned into him with a sigh of perfect contentment. Sylvia glared at him, but neither he nor her cousin noticed.

At dinnertime, he earned another glare by stealing Sylvia's seat again, just as she had known he would. She had raced for the dining room as soon as they were called to supper, and she would have beaten him, too, except that her mother had taken her aside to wash her face and hands, sticky with peppermint candy. Sylvia was stuck at the far end of the table between Uncle William and Claudia.

After dinner was served, Uncle George rose and cleared his throat. "I know it's customary for Father to make the first toast on Christmas Eve," he said, with a nod to Grandpa, "but tonight I have a very special announcement, and I think Millie might burst if we don't share our secret with you at once."

Sylvia looked at her aunt and saw to her surprise that her face shone with happiness, though her eyes brimmed with tears. Aunt Millie reached for Elizabeth's hand and held it tightly. An expectant murmur went up from the table, but Sylvia's eyes were fixed on Elizabeth as she leaned over to speak encouragingly in her mother's ear, then, with a quick smile for her friend, turned her attention to her father.

"Many of you have known Henry longer than I have since he grew up around here, and I'm sure you're all aware of what a fine young man he is." He cleared his throat. Sylvia stared. Was he going to cry? "What you may not know is that he has become like a son to me. He tells me he loves my daughter, and my daughter assures me the feeling is mutual. It must be, because he asked her to marry him and she said she would. So please join me in wishing health and happiness to the beautiful bride-to-be and the luckiest man in the world."

The joyous clamor that followed was so deafening that Sylvia stuffed her fingers in her ears. She felt ill. If Henry came to live at Elm Creek Manor, Sylvia would never have her cousin to herself. Everyone else seemed so happy, even Aunt Millie, who was crying, but Sylvia could not imagine anything worse than allowing Henry to join the family.

A few days after Christmas — a hollow, anxious day in which the joy of the season was unbearable and even the presents Santa had left beneath the tree could not lighten her heart — Sylvia discovered that there was more to Elizabeth's wedding than she could have imagined.

She was playing with her toy horses and stable, a gift from Santa, when Elizabeth came to the nursery. "Hello, Sylvia," she said, tucking her skirt beneath her as she sat on the floor beside her. "Why have you been hiding up here all alone?"

"I'm not hiding, just playing," said Sylvia. "Where's Henry?"

"He's in the stable with your father and Uncle George, looking after the horses."

Sylvia knew what that meant. If her father and uncles were willing to share the secrets of Bergstrom Thoroughbreds with Henry, they already considered him part of the family. "I don't think the horses like strangers in their stables. He should go home."

Elizabeth laughed. "Oh, Sylvia. You don't like Henry very much, do you?"

Sylvia shook her head.

"Well, I do. He's my very best friend in the world, and it would make me very happy if you could learn to like him, too. Do you think you could try?"

"I don't think so."

Elizabeth sighed and drew Sylvia onto her lap. "Please? As a special wedding present to me?"

Sylvia thought about it. "If he promises to let me sit by you sometimes at dinner. And even after he comes to live here he should go away for a little while sometimes and let us play alone the way we always do."

Elizabeth went still. "Henry isn't coming to live here," she said. "Didn't you know?"

Sylvia shook her head, suddenly hopeful. If Henry wasn't moving in, then maybe things wouldn't be so bad after all. Sylvia could pretend he and Elizabeth weren't even married.

"But the day after Christmas we explained —" Elizabeth inhaled deeply. "But maybe you were too angry to listen. Darling, Henry and I won't be living at Elm Creek Manor after the wedding."

Sylvia twisted her head to peer into her cousin's face. She knew at once that Elizabeth was not teasing her. "Where are you going to live? Close?" If Elizabeth told her they were going to live with Uncle George and Aunt Millie, Sylvia thought she might burst into tears. They lived in Pennsylvania, too, but many miles away, in Erie.

Elizabeth held her tightly. "Henry bought a ranch out in California. We'll be leaving the day after the wedding, in the spring."

Sylvia's throat closed up around her grief. She scrambled out of Elizabeth's lap and fled the room, ignoring her cousin's pleas.

Sylvia didn't want to believe that Elizabeth was telling the truth, but the other grown-ups soon confirmed it. Worse yet, the wedding was not going to take place next spring, but this coming spring, barely three months away. After discovering this, Sylvia ran to her mother and begged her to make Elizabeth change her mind.

"I couldn't even if I wished to," Sylvia's mother told her gently. "Henry and Elizabeth want to make a life for themselves out in California. We will all miss them very much, but they've made their decision."

"Can't we make them wait?" cried Sylvia. "Why do they have to get married so soon? Can't they wait until next year?"

"Why should they wait?" interrupted Claudia. "They love each other, and weddings are so beautiful. Didn't you hear, Sylvia? Elizabeth said we could be flower girls."

"I don't want to be a flower girl!"

"Well, I do, and I won't let you spoil it." Claudia tossed her head. "You're just jealous because Elizabeth likes Henry more than you."

"She does not," shouted Sylvia. "I'm her favorite. She hid the Christmas star especially for me! She put it under my pillow where no one else would find it."

Claudia's eyes narrowed. "I knew you were too little to find that star all by yourself so fast. You cheated!"

"I did not!"

"You did so. Tell her, Mama. Tell her she and Elizabeth both cheated."

"We didn't cheat. It was just helping."

"Now, girls," their mother said. "Claudia, you can see your sister is upset. Let's not make things worse."

"But it's not fair."

"We can discuss that another time."

Sylvia tugged at her mother's hand. "Will you tell Elizabeth to wait? Please?"

In reply, Sylvia's mother shook her head sadly and reached out to console her, but Sylvia broke free of her embrace and ran off to find Great-Aunt Lucinda. Everyone listened to her. If she asked Elizabeth to wait another year, Elizabeth would do it, no matter how Henry complained.

She found Lucinda in the front parlor lost in thought as she worked on her Christmas Quilt. Reluctant to annoy the only member of the family likely to help her, Sylvia crept up to her softly and sat on the floor at her feet, resting her head against the ottoman. Lucinda offered her a brief smile but kept her eyes on her work. Sylvia watched as Lucinda joined one row of star points to others she had already assembled, her needle darting through the bright fabric, in and out, joining the pieces together. Before long she tied a knot at the end of the seam and laid the finished block on her lap, pressing it flat with her palms. Sylvia was struck suddenly by the similarity between the Feathered Star blocks her great-aunt had made and the star on top of their Christmas tree, the star Elizabeth had left beneath her pillow.

Silently she counted the blocks in the pile next to her great-aunt's sewing basket, remembering to add the one on her lap. "That makes six."

"Yes, that's right. Six down, fourteen to go." With a sigh, Lucinda gathered her sewing tools and returned them to her basket. "But they will have to wait for another day."

Sylvia's heart sank, and she had not thought it could go any lower. "Why? Why are you putting it away?"

"I don't have time to work on my Christmas Quilt now that your cousin is getting married," said Lucinda. "We have so much to do, and far less than the usual time to do it. I must help your Aunt Millie make the wedding gown, and of course we must have a wedding quilt, as well as a few good, sturdy quilts for every day and all the other things your cousin will need to take with her to California."

Sylvia chose her words carefully. "Maybe if you told Elizabeth you won't have enough time to finish all the sewing, she'll wait until next year to get married."

Lucinda laughed. "Oh, I see. That's a very clever plan, but I'm afraid it won't work. Henry has his heart set on leaving as soon as fair weather arrives. We'll have a wedding at the end of March whether we like it or not, so you and I will have to make the best of it."

Sylvia felt a small stirring of hope. Great-Aunt Lucinda wasn't completely happy about the wedding, either. Perhaps Sylvia had found an ally.

But then Lucinda dashed her hopes. "Don't worry, Sylvia. We'll get to your quilting lessons soon enough."

Sylvia could not speak for her despair. Great-Aunt Lucinda thought that Sylvia cared only for her quilting lessons, and worse yet, she intended to join in on the work that would hasten cousin Elizabeth's departure.

Sylvia was on her own.

New Year's Day came. Most of the relatives returned to their own homes at the close of the Christmas season, but Elizabeth remained at Elm Creek Manor. This would have pleased Sylvia had she not known that she had stayed on for Henry, not for her favorite little cousin. Sylvia kept close to Elizabeth when her fiancé was not around, but as soon as he showed up, Sylvia ran off to the nursery or to the west sitting room, where her mother often sat reading or simply enjoying the afternoon sun and the view of Elm Creek. Her mother had a weak heart, the lingering consequence of a childhood bout with rheumatic fever. She often had to rest, but she was never too tired to offer Sylvia a hug or tell her a story.

But as the winter snows melted and buds began to form on the elm trees surrounding the manor, even her mother became so caught up in the preparations for the wedding that she had little time to comfort a sulky daughter.

On one rare occasion when Sylvia and Elizabeth were alone, Sylvia asked her, "Why do you want to go away from home?"

"You'll understand someday, little Sylvia." Elizabeth smiled and hugged her, but there were tears in her eyes. "Someday you'll fall in love, and you'll know that home is wherever he is."

"Home is here," Sylvia insisted. "It will always be here."

Elizabeth gave a little laugh and held her close. "Yes, Sylvia, you're right."

Happily, Sylvia realized that finally her cousin had come to her senses and had decided to stay. But when Elizabeth rose and ran off to the sitting room when Aunt Millie called her to a dress fitting, Sylvia's joy fled. Elizabeth intended to marry Henry, even though it was obvious she did not really wish to leave home. It was all his fault; Elizabeth wouldn't be going anywhere if not for him.

Sylvia realized that the only way to keep Elizabeth close was to drive Henry away.

From that moment on, Sylvia did all she could to prevent the wedding. She hid Aunt Millie's scissors so that she could not work on the wedding gown, but Aunt Millie simply borrowed Lucinda's. She stole the keys to Elizabeth's red steamer trunk and flung them into Elm Creek so that she could not pack her belongings. She refused to try on her flower girl dress no matter how the aunts wheedled and coaxed, until they were forced to make a pattern from the frock she had worn on Christmas. In one last, desperate effort, she told Henry that she hated him, that he was not allowed to sit in her chair at the dinner table ever again, and that everyone in the family including Elizabeth wished he would just go away, but they were too polite to say it.

Her efforts were entirely unsuccessful, of course. In late March, Elizabeth and Henry married and moved to California. Sylvia treasured every letter her beloved cousin sent her, even as they appeared less and less frequently over the years, until they finally stopped coming.

Sylvia never saw Elizabeth again. She often wondered what had become of her, why she had stopped writing. If Claudia had kept in touch with Elizabeth or her descendants, Sylvia had found no record of their correspondence in her sister's papers.

Sarah interrupted her reverie. "What do you think?" she asked, admiring her arrangement of the various pieces of the Christmas Quilt and looking to Sylvia for approval.

Sylvia dared not look at the quilt blocks for fear of what other memories they would call forth. "I think it's time to finish decorating." She rose from her chair and left the room without waiting to see if Sarah followed.

Chapter Two

A few minutes later, Sarah joined Sylvia in the foyer, where Sylvia had busied herself sorting the dining room linens from decorations that belonged elsewhere in the manor. "I couldn't reach Matt on the cell phone to remind him to bring home a tree," said Sarah. "We might have to cut down our own after all."

"Suit yourself."

"I'd prefer to suit all of us."

"Since I don't care one way or the other, whatever suits you will be fine with me." Sylvia stooped over to pick up a napkin holder shaped like a sprig of ivy. Once it had belonged to a set of twenty-four, but Sylvia would be satisfied if she could find three, one for each of the current residents of Elm Creek Manor. It was a pity they had decided not to run their quilters' retreat all year instead of only March through October. A dozen or so quilt campers certainly would liven up the place, and with their help, she and Sarah would make quick work of all the decorating Sarah apparently still had her heart set on, despite the new distraction of the quilt.

"Decorating the entire manor seems too ambitious considering our late start," said Sylvia. "Why don't we concentrate on only those rooms we use the most?"

Sarah mulled over the suggestion as if uncertain whether it was a practical idea or a plot to keep her from decorating as lavishly as she wished. "I guess that's a good idea," she said, clearly reluctant to abandon her original vision. "What rooms do you suggest?"

"The foyer, of course, since we have already begun, and to make a good impression on any visitors."

"Were you expecting visitors?"

"No, but one never knows at this time of the year." And one could always hope. Perhaps some of the Elm Creek Quilters might drop by if they found a lull in their family activities. "We could invite your mother."

"No way. Not a good idea."

On the contrary, it was a wonderful idea, such a perfect solution that Sylvia could have kicked herself for not thinking of it sooner. "Why on earth not?"

"For one reason, among many, I'm sure she's made other plans by now."

Sylvia doubted it. Sarah was Carol Mallory's only child, and she had sent at least one letter asking Sarah to come home. She had also phoned twice that Sylvia knew of. "If she has made other plans, she's free to decline our invitation, but at the very least we ought to give her that opportunity."

"It's too late," Sarah insisted. "Even if she could drop everything the moment we call, she would still have to pack and make that long drive. She wouldn't arrive until late tonight. We'd have Christmas morning together, but she'd have to leave by mid-afternoon so she can be home at a reasonable hour. She has to get up early for work the next day."

"How do you know she has to work?"

"She always works the day after Christmas," said Sarah flatly. "She always takes the early shift at the hospital to give another nurse the chance to take the day off. My mother would rather take the overtime than sleep in. It's our own family Christmas tradition."

Thinking of how long Sarah's widowed mother had been the sole provider for their small family, Sylvia said, "Perhaps it was a matter of needing rather than merely wanting the overtime."

"I don't know. Maybe. She could have taken it any other day, though. Why take it the day after Christmas, when I was on school break and all my friends were busy with their families?"

Despite the sympathy evoked by images of a young Sarah left alone at home on the day after Christmas, Sylvia shook her head in disapproval. Sarah seemed incapable of seeing anything from her mother's point of view. She claimed it was too late to invite Carol to come for Christmas, but anyone with any sense could see she was just making excuses.

Sarah had turned away and had busied herself with sorting through a box of Christmas stocking hangers the Bergstroms had once lined up on the fireplace mantel each St. Nicholas Day. "After the foyer, where else should we decorate?"

Sylvia muffled a sigh, recognizing Sarah's attempt to change the subject but unwilling to pursue the matter. "The west sitting room. Perhaps we can move the armchair and set up the tree in the corner."

"Is that where your family usually put it up?"

"No, we used the ballroom, but in those days we needed the extra space to accommodate family and guests. The west sitting room would be much cozier for the three of us." The ballroom had been subdivided into classrooms for the quilt camp, too, and Sylvia didn't relish moving all of the partitions.

Sarah nodded and gestured toward the red-and-green tartan table linens. "What about the dining room?"

"Oh, let's decorate the kitchen and eat there as we always do. The tablecloth will look just as festive on our usual table."

Sarah agreed, and as she gathered up the linens, Sylvia collected three of the holly napkin rings and picked up the Santa Claus cookie jar. They carried everything to the kitchen, one of the few rooms in the older wing of the house that Claudia had kept up with the times, more or less. The spacious room was painted a maple sugar hue that made the most of the afternoon sunlight, with the help of a copper light fixture that reminded Sylvia of an old-fashioned carriage lantern. It was suspended over the long wooden table and benches that filled the space between the doorway and the kitchen proper. Cupboards and appliances lined the walls except for the window over the sink, the door to the pantry in the southwest corner, and the open doorway that led to the west sitting room. A small microwave sat on the countertop beside the old gas oven Sylvia had cooked upon even before her abrupt departure so many years ago; it was a marvel of pre–World War II technology that it still worked at all. The refrigerator on the opposite wall appeared fairly new, perhaps less than ten years old, but the printed curtains had last been in style in the 1970s. The dishwasher Sarah had insisted they install stood out proudly, its gleaming stainless-steel finish intimidating every other appliance in the room. The kitchen was such a mishmash of old and new that Sylvia couldn't bear to change any of it, even though she knew it was not up to the standards of a professional kitchen and would prove hopelessly inadequate if their quilt camp grew at the pace Sarah predicted.

Sarah wiped off the long wooden table and draped the red-and-green tartan tablecloth over it. She placed two candlesticks in the center as Sylvia took clean cloth napkins from a drawer and tucked them into the holly wreath rings. Then Sylvia put the Santa Claus cookie jar between the candlesticks and declared that it made a fine centerpiece.

"Too bad it isn't full," remarked Sarah, lifting the lid to be sure.

"Even your sweet tooth couldn't handle fifty-year-old cookies," teased Sylvia, easing herself onto one of the benches. Images filled her mind, she and Claudia and her cousins swinging their feet as they sat on the bench dunking cookies into milk and leaving scuffmarks on the wooden floor with their shoes. A quick glance told her that time had worn away most of those marks, but some remained. She resisted the impulse to trace them with her fingertips.

"Maybe we should drive out to the bakery and fill it up with Christmas cookies," suggested Sarah.

"If you could find a bakery open on Christmas Eve, and if I thought you could do it without sending my great-aunt Lucinda spinning in her grave. Store-bought cookies in her favorite cookie jar? My dear, that's close to sacrilege in this house."

Sarah sat down on the opposite bench, amused. "I suppose you Bergstroms insisted upon homemade cookies."

"When you had a baker like Great-Aunt

Lucinda in the family, you couldn't tolerate anything less. She made all the good German Christmas cookies precisely the way her mother had taught her. Lebkuchen — that's gingerbread; she made hers with grated almonds and candied orange peel. Aniseed cookies called anisplätzchen, and zimtsterne, cinnamon stars. She tried to keep that cookie jar filled from St. Nicholas Day through the Feast of the Three Kings, but we children ate them as fast as she could bake. It's no wonder she left the apple strudel to the other bakers in the family."

"I made apple strudel once," remarked Sarah. "You take the phyllo dough out of the box and place it on a cookie sheet, open up a can of apple pie filling, spread it all around, roll it up and bake it."

Sylvia cast her gaze to heaven. "Your generation will be forever remembered for its culinary ignorance."

"It was delicious," protested Sarah. "Especially with a little vanilla frosting on top."

"That is not strudel," said Sylvia. "Not real strudel, at any rate. If you had ever tasted my mother's, even your damaged taste buds would perceive the difference."

"I'm willing to learn. Teach me how to

make the real thing."

Sylvia waved a hand, dismissing the notion. "I haven't made it since the war — the Second World War, before you get the idea that it was more recent. I would need at least a day to try to re-create the recipe from memory."

"You mean it isn't written down?"

"Of course not, dear. In those days, an accomplished cook didn't measure cups and teaspoonfuls; it was a heaping handful of flour here, a dash of salt there, bake in a hot oven until done. The instructions were never as specific as cooks require today."

And yet somehow food had always tasted better then, when recipes were handed down from mother to daughter and stored in one's memory rather than in a card file or on a computer.

From down the hall, she heard the back door slam; a moment later, Sarah's husband appeared in the doorway carrying two paper grocery sacks. "Looks nice," he remarked, admiring the festive table. "Does this mean Christmas isn't canceled after all?"

"Not even Sylvia can cancel Christmas," said Sarah. "No one can."

"Oliver Cromwell did," remarked Sylvia, rising and taking one of the bags from

Matt. "In the 1640s, when he came to power in England. He thought it was too decadent. But I'm no Oliver Cromwell, and Christmas at Elm Creek Manor was never canceled. You shouldn't make assumptions based upon the lack of paper snowflakes and strings of colored lights. One doesn't need decorations to have Christmas."

"But it helps." To Matt, Sarah added, "Let's go out soon and get a tree. To me, it doesn't feel like Christmas unless it looks like Christmas."

"And sounds like Christmas," replied Matt. "We need to put on some carols."

"I left my CD player in the foyer," Sarah told him. He left the second bag of groceries on the counter and went to retrieve it, his curly blond head just clearing the doorframe. While they waited, Sylvia and Sarah put away the groceries Matt had purchased for their Christmas dinner, including sweet potatoes, cranberries, corn, apples, flour, onions, celery, and a contraband can of gravy Sylvia had deliberately crossed off the shopping list. Honestly. Canned gravy at Elm Creek Manor for Christmas dinner. When Sarah was not looking, Sylvia hid the gravy in a back corner of the pantry so that she would have no choice but to allow Sylvia to make theirs from scratch. Everything else they needed, they already had on hand. A turkey breast was defrosting on the bottom shelf of the refrigerator, and Sylvia had already torn a loaf of bread into cubes for the stuffing. She had made a pumpkin pie earlier that morning, before the young people came down for breakfast.

Sarah and Matt were quite right to attribute the holiday feeling to the sights and sounds of the season, but it was the smells and tastes of Christmas that flooded Sylvia with memories, transporting her to Christmases past as if she had lived those moments only yesterday and not decades ago. When Sylvia caught the scent of aniseed, no matter where she was or what the season, her thoughts immediately turned to Great-Aunt Lucinda, turning out batches of savory cookies for her eager nieces and nephews. The smell of baking apples and cinnamon and pastry called to mind her mother, and her grandmother, and even her great-grandfather's sister, Gerda Bergstrom, the first to make strudel in the kitchen of the farmhouse that would one day become Elm Creek Manor.

Gerda Bergstrom had brought the strudel recipe over from Germany when she emigrated in the 1850s; all of the family stories agreed upon that. Whether she had created it herself or learned it from her mother, no one knew. Either way, everyone who tasted Gerda's strudel affirmed that it was the most delicious they had ever tasted: the apples perfectly sliced and flavored with sugar and cinnamon, the pastry flaky and as light as air. Only a privileged few were ever treated to her strudel, and only at yuletide. All year she scrimped and saved her butter and egg money so that come December, she would have enough to purchase all the ingredients for the number of strudel she intended to make that year. She always made two for the family, which were devoured in a matter of minutes at breakfast Christmas morning. The others, sometimes as many as two dozen, she gave as gifts to her friends and to others whom she did not know as well, but who had earned her gratitude for a particular kindness they had shown her in the past year. Only one family other than her own received two strudels without fail every season: Dr. Jonathan Granger's, most likely because his services were so necessary and his friendship so valuable in a town with only one doctor. "I give you simply the joy and hope of the season," she would say as she offered a strudel to the lucky recipient, but neither the act nor the gift was as simple as she professed. Come Christmas Eve, when Gerda drove her brother's horse and wagon from farm to farm and through the streets of their small town distributing her gifts, everyone knew exactly where they stood with her. Some were pleasantly surprised; others ruefully resolved to be friendlier toward the outspoken spinster in the year to come.

As an unmarried woman living in her brother's household, Gerda would have been determined not to become a burden. By all accounts she was a hard worker, cooking for the family and tending her brother's children so her sister-in-law, a skilled seamstress, could earn extra money taking in sewing. Her strudel was already famous throughout the Elm Creek Valley by the time her nieces were old enough to learn her secrets. Later, when her nephews married, she taught their wives. Still, while every Bergstrom woman followed her instructions to the letter with results that would have been applauded in any other family, everyone agreed that Gerda's strudel remained unmatched in every regard.

After Gerda died, her cooking took on legendary attributes. More than one young bride marrying into the Bergstrom family fled to her room in tears after the strudel she had labored over for hours met with approving nods from her in-laws and fond reminiscences of the far superior crust or the more sublimely spiced apples Gerda had prepared long ago. Younger generations could only listen enviously as their elders recollected the Christmas feasts Gerda had created single-handedly in a kitchen that for most of her life boasted only a wood-burning stove and a root cellar. Once Sylvia was sent to her room for wondering aloud why Gerda could not have found any more productive use for her time than to haunt the kitchen peeling apples and stretching dough day and night, for that's what she must have done in order to produce as many pastries as family legend would have it.

But even though none could equal Gerda in the kitchen, every Bergstrom woman who learned her secret recipe had been armed with the power to win the admiration of young men, the respect of future mothers-in-law, and the envy of the other women whose family had been fortunate enough to receive a gift of the famous Bergstrom strudel.

Then a time came when so many women of the family knew how to make it that the next generation could not be bothered to learn. Why should they, when another aunt or cousin could be relied upon to make one for the family's Christmas breakfast and the several others necessary to fulfill Gerda's tradition of giving them away to the dearest friends of the family? It went unnoticed that, with each aged aunt who passed on or each young wife who moved away with her new husband, a little of Gerda's knowledge vanished into history.

Sylvia's mother was fortunate to learn from several of those who had been taught by Gerda herself: her mother-in-law and two of her husband's aunts, Lydia and Lucinda. Eleanor must have mastered the recipe quickly, for in Sylvia's earliest memories of watching the women of her family labor in the kitchen, her mother could handle the fragile dough as expertly as any Bergstrom-born.

Eleanor was also a talented quilter, but not only because of the Bergstroms' tutelage. She had learned to quilt as a child in New York City, and one of her most treasured possessions was the Crazy Quilt she had made with the help of her beloved nanny. When she first joined her husband's family at Elm Creek Manor, she had impressed the other women with her equal skill in patchwork and appliqué, whereas the Bergstrom women tended to favor one or the other. There were other differences; none of the Bergstroms had ever made a Crazy Quilt, a heavily embroidered, often delicate work created more for decoration than warmth, and they frequently knew the same patterns by different names. Over the years, they shared their knowledge and each woman considered her store richer for the collaboration.

Sylvia must have been seven or eight when Eleanor found Great-Aunt Lucinda's Feathered Star blocks tucked away in the family scrap bag with the leftover green and red fabrics. "These are too finely made to use for scraps," Eleanor protested when Lucinda explained that they had not found their way into the bag by mistake, for she had discarded them years ago. Her eyes were not as strong as they had once been, and she no longer felt capable of piecing together the tiny triangles as precisely as necessary. One of the aunts proposed stitching together the six blocks Lucinda had completed into a crib quilt, but after some discussion, all agreed that the eighteen-inch blocks were too large and overpowering to suit a baby's coverlet. Eventually Eleanor decided to continue making a full-size Christmas quilt, but rather than create additional Feathered Stars that would be compared to Lucinda's, she would appliqué holly wreaths and plumes to frame the older woman's work.

Eleanor worked on the quilt more consistently than Lucinda had, stitching the green holly leaves and deep red berries to ivory squares of fabric with tiny, meticulous stitches throughout the year. But although she did not put away the quilt at the end of the Christmas season, she progressed more slowly than Lucinda, for she could sew only for an hour or two at a time before headaches and fatigue forced her to set her handwork aside. Her health, which had never been robust, had begun a slow and steady decline after the birth of her youngest child and only son. Her condition had worsened markedly after the deaths of her mother and mother-in-law, less than a year apart. One by one she relinquished the activities she had once enjoyed: horseback riding, strolls along Elm Creek with Sylvia's father, picnics and games in the north gardens. The aunts took over her household duties without alluding to the necessity for Eleanor to rest. Her love for her family shone as strongly as ever, defying the weakness of her body, so that the children sometimes almost forgot her infirmity. She was their beloved Mama. It did not really matter whether she played with them, or if she merely held them on her lap and told them stories. They were happy in her company.

When December snows began to fall in Sylvia's ninth year, she offered to help her mother finish the Christmas Quilt in time for the holiday. She had recently finished a floral appliqué sampler and had improved her stitches so much that she was eager to take on a more important project. Her mother agreed, adding with a rueful laugh that without Sylvia's help, she might be obliged to give up as Lucinda had done.

Sylvia could not bear the thought of that, not after her mother had worked so hard to create such beautiful holly wreaths and sprays, so lifelike that Sylvia half-expected them to stir in the breeze. To spare her mother the effort, she traced her mother's leaf template onto stiff paper, cut out the shapes, paired them with pieces of green fabric, and basted the raw edges down until the fabric conformed to the paper. To make the berries, she placed a dime on the wrong side of a circle of fabric a quarter inch larger in diameter, then held the dime in place as she took small running stitches in the fabric circle all the way around the edge, leaving longer thread tails at the beginning and the end. She gently pulled the threads, drawing the fabric circle around the dime, and pressed with a hot iron. After loosening the threads to slip out the coin, she basted the edges of the fabric into a circle the size of a dime with perfectly smooth edges. All that remained for her mother to do was baste the leaves and berries in place on the background fabric and appliqué them securely.

Even with Sylvia's help, her mother tired easily and often rested with her sewing on her lap, watching two-year-old Richard play or supervising Claudia as she strung popcorn, berries, and nuts for the Christmas tree. Uncle William and his wife had needed four hours to choose a tree the previous year, which according to Sylvia's father was a new record. The delay forced the family to rush to finish decorating the tree before bedtime. Sylvia had overheard some speculation that Uncle William and his bride had not spent all that time searching for a tree, but she could not imagine what else they might have been doing out there all alone in the snowy woods. Maybe they had gotten lost. In any event, Claudia was determined to be ready for an even longer search this year by preparing the decorations in advance.

Two days before Christmas, Great-Aunt Lydia announced her intention to make apple strudel that day, and anyone who wished to help would be welcome. Despite her weariness, Sylvia's mother took an interest. "How many do you plan to make?" she asked.

"Four," said Lydia. "One for us and three for the usual friends."

"Only four?" asked Eleanor. The family's interest in Gerda's tradition had diminished over the years as they had found other ways to express their affection and gratitude to their friends and neighbors. Quilted and knitted gifts were popular, but Sylvia had overheard Great-Aunt Lucinda tell Lydia that most families in the Elm Creek Valley would be grateful to find coal in their stockings this year. "Aunt Gerda always said the simple gifts were best," she had added, "but this year, simple is all most folks will be able to manage, and joy and hope may be in short supply."

They had been careful to speak of such things out of Eleanor's hearing, and now, confronted with her surprise, Lucinda and Lydia exchanged a look and Sylvia grew still. Her father and the other adults did their best to shield Eleanor and the children from distressing news, but Sylvia had perfected the art of eavesdropping on her elders. She knew what concerned her aunts, even if she did not entirely understand the cause. In October, the First Bank of Waterford had lost all the family's money along with the savings of its other customers. For reasons that did not seem fair to Sylvia, a larger bank in a far-off city had called in a debt and had cleared out the Waterford bank vault in order to pay its own customers. Her father said that this was happening throughout the nation — banks failing, factories closing, everywhere men losing their means of earning a living. Rich men leaped to their deaths from skyscrapers rather than endure bankruptcy, and poor men sold apples on street corners.

Sylvia's mother knew what was happening around the country because the family could not hide the newspaper or turn off the radio without explaining why. What she did not know — what her husband had tried to conceal from her — was how seriously their own family had been affected. Eleanor did not know that their savings had been lost, or that the family business had not generated any income for months. The wealth of most of their former customers had been wiped out in the stock market crash. No one had the money to spend on luxuries like expensive horses. The Bergstroms would get by because they were moderately self-sufficient; they owned their own land and thus did not have to pay a mortgage, and they grew some of their own food. They had ample wood from their forest to heat the home if their supply of coal ran out before spring. The manor was full of desirable possessions they could use to pay off Eleanor's doctor bills and barter for whatever else they needed in town. But for the first time since Gerda Bergstrom's day, the family had to watch every penny. Lydia's expenditures on white flour, sugar, and cinnamon, a trifle any other Christmas, had already led to one argument with some of the men of the household.

"These are difficult times," Lydia tried to explain, reluctant to burden Eleanor with worries.

"And they will worsen before they improve," said Eleanor firmly, setting her quilting aside. "All the more reason for those of us who have been blessed to share our abundance with others."

The look of concern and dismay the other adults shared was so obvious Sylvia did not see how her mother could have misunderstood its meaning, but of course, Eleanor had no idea how much their abundance had dwindled. When she called for Sylvia to help her from her chair, Sylvia hurried to her mother's side and steadied her as she stood. On her feet, Eleanor looked around the circle of worried faces. "Will any of you help me?" When none of the aunts replied, Eleanor's mouth tightened almost imperceptibly. "Very well. Sylvia, would you?" Sylvia nodded. "That's a good girl. And you, Claudia?" More solemnly, Claudia nodded. "Good. It's time you girls tried your hand at Gerda's recipe anyway. You're old enough to do more than peel apples."

As Eleanor and her daughters left the parlor, Lydia opened her mouth to speak, but any protest she might have intended was abruptly silenced by a gesture from Lucinda. No one followed them down the hall to the kitchen, where Eleanor pulled out the bench and sat down at the table rather than standing at the counter as she used to do. She called for her mixing bowl, for flour, water, salt, and butter; Sylvia and Claudia scrambled to set everything before her. Their mother's mouth turned in a frown when she saw the limp flour sack, and Sylvia knew she was measuring with her eyes and calculating how far it would go.

"It will have to do," she murmured with a sigh. She ordered Claudia to fetch two eggs from the barn. She would make up the pastry dough two at a time and make as many as their larder would allow.

"Remember this, girls," their mother instructed when Claudia returned. She reached into the flour sack and put six large handfuls into her mixing bowl. She tossed in a pinch of salt, blended the two, and made a well in the center with a spoon. Into this she added an egg, a cup of water, and a dollop of fresh butter, which Sylvia brought to her. With both hands she mixed everything together, working in silence. Sylvia and Claudia exchanged a look, a silent warning not to speak, not to warn their mother that this was the last of the flour, that salt was scarce, that Great-Aunt Lucinda had been trading the eggs with neighboring farmers for sausage and ham. Sylvia was not sure it would have made a difference.

Eleanor turned the dough out onto a floured board and began kneading, the hard line of her mouth gradually relaxing as she worked. After a few minutes she called Claudia to take a turn squeezing, pressing, and folding the dough over and over again. Next Sylvia took a turn, kneading the dough until her hands and shoulders grew tired. Her mother took over for her, working the dough expertly with the heels of her hands.

"When I was a little girl," she said suddenly, "my parents employed a French chef who made *bûche de noël* for our Christmas dessert. Do you know what that is? It's a cake rolled and shaped to look like a yule log. He decorated it with chocolate frosting and meringue mushrooms. It was such a treat. My sister and I looked forward to it all year."

"Didn't your mother make strudel?" asked Sylvia.

Her mother laughed. "My mother? Oh, no, darling. My mother did not cook. I didn't taste strudel until I married your father and came to live here."

"Maybe we could make a yule log cake sometime," said Claudia.

"Perhaps someday. I prefer Bergstrom ways."

The dough had become a smooth, satiny ball beneath their mother's capable hands. She divided it into halves, separated them on the floured board, and covered them with a dishtowel. "Now we let the dough rest while we prepare the apples."

"We'll get them," said Sylvia quickly, motioning for Claudia to follow her down to the cellar. The apples, harvested from their own orchard and stored below where in winter it was as cold as the icebox, were heaped in bushel baskets along one wall, as red and crisp as the day they were picked. Choosing the nearest basket, each girl seized a handle and lugged the apples upstairs. Their mother sat up quickly and smiled when they returned, but it was obvious she had been resting her head on the table.

Sylvia fetched three paring knives from the drawer and sat down on the bench across from her mother and sister. Eleanor could peel three apples as swiftly as Sylvia peeled one, the red skin rolling off in a continuous, narrow ribbon as thin as paper. Sylvia tried to imitate her, but her strips usually broke as soon as they became long enough to touch her lap, and thick chunks of juicy white apple flesh sometimes came off with the peel. Eleanor wielded the paring knife so deftly that it was impossible to believe that she had not been preparing apples for strudel since she was Sylvia's age, or that she had ever spent Christmas anywhere but here.

"Mama?" asked Sylvia, forgetting her promise not to tire her mother with too many questions. "What was Christmas like when you were my age?"

"Very much like it is today," her mother said after a moment. "It was a day for celebrating the Lord's birth, for family, for special treats, beautiful carols, and if we had been very good girls, a visit from Santa Claus."

As piles of apple peelings collected on the table and their fingers grew sticky with juice, their mother told them stories of Christmases in New York — of fancy balls, concerts in the city, the annual trip to her father's department store on Fifth Avenue where she and her sister were allowed to choose any toy they wanted. She spoke more warmly of quieter celebrations in the nursery with her English nanny, who taught her about Christmas ghost stories and Christmas crackers and their obligation to help those in need, especially during the holidays but throughout the year. Sylvia wondered if the nanny's lessons accounted for her mother's determination to continue Gerda Bergstrom's tradition of giving.

When Eleanor decided they had peeled enough apples, her storytelling ceased. She demonstrated how to slice and cut the fruit into uniform pieces, once again finishing three apples to their every one. She sent Claudia to the linen closet for a freshly laundered sheet while she and Sylvia scooped the apple slices into a bowl and mixed them with two heaping handfuls of bread crumbs, a sprinkling of cinnamon, two handfuls of sugar, finely chopped walnuts, and a large spoonful of softened butter. The sweet smell of apples and cinnamon was too much for Sylvia, and she could not resist dipping her finger into the bowl to taste the sweet juice that had collected at the bottom.

"What do you think, girls?" their mother asked when Claudia returned from upstairs. "Has the dough rested sufficiently?" Sylvia did not know how to judge, but Claudia answered yes so confidently that Sylvia quickly chimed in her agreement rather than appear to know less than her sister. After the girls wiped the table clean, their mother covered the table with the sheet, pulled it smooth, and secured it in place with clothespins. She dusted the sheet with flour, but Sylvia noticed that she used far less than in previous years.

Eleanor instructed her daughters to wash their hands; when they returned from the sink, fingers freshly scrubbed and patted dry, they found her rolling out one of the dough balls into a rectangle in the center of the floured sheet. When she could roll the dough no thinner with the rolling pin, she set it aside. "Watch carefully," she instructed her daughters. "Someday you will need to know how to do this on your own."

She slipped her hands beneath the dough rectangle and gently stretched it, pulling carefully with the backs of her hands and her thumbs and allowing the dough to fall back upon the floured cloth. Stepping around to another side of the table, she repeated the motions until she had walked all the way around the table and stretched the dough on all four sides. "This will go faster if you two help me," she remarked, reaching beneath the pastry dough again. "And I won't have to walk around the table so many times."

Sylvia flushed with nervousness and pride as she took her place on the other side of the table from her mother. She had often watched her mother, aunts, and older cousins stretching the dough, but she and Claudia had never been permitted to join in. The fragile dough must be stretched to a uniform tissue-paper thinness everywhere, with no tears and no thicker patches to ruin the delicate texture. Sylvia's touch was at first tentative, but then as she saw how the dough responded as she gently drew it from the center out, she grew bolder.

"Mama," Claudia exclaimed just as Sylvia saw what she had done. "Sylvia tore a hole."

Mortified, Sylvia pulled her hands free of the dough and allowed it to fall to the table. A three-inch maw in the dough glared up at her.

"That's all right," said Eleanor, hurrying over. "It's easily mended." She gently pinched the tear closed and smiled reassuringly at Sylvia, but the seam was too visible and she knew she had ruined the strudel.

"I'm sorry, Mama," she said. What would the aunts say when they found out?

"Don't worry, darling," said Eleanor. "I imagine even Gerda Bergstrom tore the dough from time to time. When your grandmother first taught me to make it, I tore the dough so many times that it looked like a sweater the moths had found. We patched every hole and the strudel was still delicious, and I'm sure this one will be, too."

Sylvia felt better, but Claudia shook her head in silent disgust. Leave it to the careless little sister to ruin the Bergstrom reputation, her look seemed to say.

Eleanor urged her daughters back to the task. Sylvia obeyed, but more cautiously this time. Gradually the dough grew longer and wider until it was nearly translucent. Eventually the dough stretched to the edges of the table, impossibly thin. Their mother circled the table one last time, trimming off the thicker edges with a knife. She set the scraps aside — she would make soup noodles with them later — and beckoned for Sylvia to bring her the apple slices. While Sylvia held the bowl, Eleanor scooped out the apples and lined one long edge of the dough from one end of the table to the other, piling up the slices in the shape of a log.

When she had finished, Eleanor set the empty bowl on the counter, her face flushed. Worried, Sylvia watched her while she held on to the back of a chair to rest, but she paused only a moment. Then, starting at one end, she carefully folded the dough over the apples until they could not be seen. "This is where teamwork is essential, girls," she said, unclipping two of the clothespins. Her daughters had helped with this part before and knew what was to come. They took their places on either side of their mother and grasped the long edge of the sheet with both hands. Eleanor counted to three, and then they lifted the sheet so that the log of apples rolled away from them, wrapping itself up in dough as it went. Eleanor bent the strudel into a horseshoe, put it in a pan, and brushed it with butter left to melt on the stovetop. Claudia helped her slide the pan into the oven, and then, Sylvia thought with relief, they were finished.

"Well done, girls," their mother praised. "But the proof will be in the tasting."

Sylvia's mouth watered in anticipation, but she knew they would have to wait until breakfast Christmas morning to enjoy the fruit of their labors. Eleanor allowed them to savor their moment of pride for only a moment before reminding them of the second ball of dough waiting to be stretched. A few minutes before the second strudel was ready to shape for the pan, the first had finished cooking. The heavenly aroma of cinnamon apples poured into the kitchen as Eleanor opened the oven door and took out the baking pan. To Sylvia's joy, it looked exactly as it should, exactly like every strudel the Bergstrom women had made in that kitchen for generations.

With the second strudel in the oven, Sylvia was eager to begin another. "Shall we get more apples from the cellar, Mama?"

"Let's rest a while first," said Claudia, her eyes on their mother's face.

"Or you could allow us to help," remarked Great-Aunt Lucinda from the doorway. Great-Aunt Lydia peeked in over her shoulder, nodding.

"She asked you to help before and you refused," said Sylvia.

"Hush, darling," said her mother gently. She smiled at the aunts. "We'd be glad for your help. Many hands make light work."

As their more experienced aunts joined in, Sylvia and Claudia were reduced to their usual role of kitchen helpers. They fetched utensils and ingredients for their elders, provided an extra hand here or quick clean-up there, but mostly, they watched and they listened. Sylvia drank in their stories of Christmases from long ago, of the hardships and the joys the women of her family experienced within those walls. Her mother listened, too, peeling apples slowly and steadily in her chair, her face no longer flushed, but pale, her smile content but weary.

By late afternoon the flour sack was empty and the sugar bin nearly so, but fourteen flaky, golden brown strudel lay side by side on the wooden table. Lucinda and Lydia promptly turned their attention to their delayed dinner preparations while Sylvia and Claudia cleaned up the mess. Their mother rose to assist, but Lucinda encouraged her to go upstairs and lie down for a while. "I can't rest with so much yet to do before Christmas," she protested, but when the aunts insisted, she agreed to sit in the front parlor and work on the Christmas Quilt until they needed her.

Naturally, Lucinda and Lydia had no intention of calling her until the men came in and the meal was served. Even Sylvia knew that. She tried to listen in on the aunts' hushed conversation as she picked up apple peelings and washed dishes, catching words and phrases that convinced her they were discussing Eleanor's strange insistence upon baking so many strudel, more than the Bergstroms had made for gifts in years. But the elder women kept their voices deliberately low so that Sylvia learned nothing, not even what they planned to tell the men when they had no flour to bake bread the next day.

Due to their haste or, just as likely, the contents of the larder, dinner was a simple affair of biscuits left over from breakfast and sausages, apples, and onions fried up together in Grandmother's enormous cast-iron pan. Great-Aunt Lucinda told Claudia to set the dining room table while Sylvia went to the parlor to summon her mother. She found her asleep in the armchair, holly leaf appliqués scattered on her lap, thimble still on her finger.

If the men of the family were surprised to discover fourteen strudels displayed on the kitchen table, they said nothing of it at dinner. Maybe, Sylvia hoped, they had not gone into the kitchen at all. Maybe they would stay away until the pastries were wrapped in wax paper, tied with ribbon, and safely tucked away out of sight in baskets, ready for delivery. By an unspoken agreement, the women said nothing of how Sylvia's mother had spent her day. Throughout the meal, Sylvia found herself nervously waiting for her mother to divulge the truth, but Eleanor spoke little. As soon as dinner was finished, she excused herself and went upstairs to bed.

As soon as she was out of earshot, the men revealed that they were well aware of the secret. Uncle William criticized their wastefulness, while Sylvia's father wondered angrily why they had allowed Eleanor to work herself so hard.

"We couldn't have stopped her," said Lucinda. "Not without a good reason, not without divulging the truth about our finances. I don't even know if that would have convinced her."

"But you used up the last of the flour," said Uncle William.

"I have eggs to trade for more."

"We encouraged her to rest," added Lydia. "Most of the time she was simply sitting, peeling apples."

"Obviously that was enough to exhaust her." Sylvia's father rose and shoved in his chair, and only then did he seem to remember his three children still seated at the table, hanging on every word. Even two-year-old Richard looked solemn and anxious. "But she'll be fine after a good night's rest."

Sylvia knew her father had added the last for their benefit. She wanted to believe him.

The next morning, Sylvia came downstairs to breakfast to find her mother in the kitchen packing the strudel carefully into baskets. She was shaking her head in mild exasperation as her husband tried to coax her back to bed. "I am not tired, and I am not about to linger in bed on the morning of Christmas Eve," she told him. "I need to take these around to the neighbors now so that I'll return before we send William and Nellie out to find a tree. I don't want to miss that."

"At least let me drive you," Sylvia's father persisted.

Eleanor stopped packing the baskets and looked him squarely in the eye. "Freddy, in all these years you have never treated me like an invalid and I forbid you to start now. You cannot protect me from what is coming, but you can make this time more bearable. Don't bury me before I've passed."

The anger in her mother's gentle voice shocked Sylvia. "Mama?"

Her father turned his head toward her with a jerk, but her mother looked up more slowly, as if she was not surprised to discover Sylvia in the doorway. "What is it, darling?"

"What's coming? You said something is coming. I heard you."

Her mother said nothing.

"Christmas," her father said abruptly. "Christmas is coming. Have you forgotten what day it is?"

Sylvia shook her head, both in response to his question and in rejection of his false reply. "Mama?" she said again, pleading. "Why are you angry at Daddy?"

Her mother hesitated. "Because I know he's right." She forced a smile, but Sylvia saw tears in her eyes. "I do work myself too hard sometimes, especially at this time of year. Freddy, I accept your offer to drive me. Thank you. Sylvia, would you come along, too, and help me give out the famous Bergstrom strudel to our friends? It's only fitting, since you helped make them."

"Of course, Mama," said Sylvia, forcing cheer into her voice. Silently she chastised herself for not heeding her father's wishes. How many times had he warned the children not to tire their mother? If Sylvia and Claudia had not agreed to help their mother make strudel, perhaps she would have stayed in her chair in the parlor, sewing on the Christmas Quilt and conserving her strength. Or perhaps she would have made the strudel alone, exhausting her last reserves of energy and rendering herself bedridden. Sylvia could not be sure if they had done right or wrong in helping their mother. It was all so confusing and strange. For years the adults of the family had cautioned the children that their mother was not well and that they should let her rest. Sometimes they forgot, but mostly they did as they were told. What good had it done? Quiet rest, visits from the doctor, concealing the truth about their finances — none of it made any difference as far as Sylvia could see. When was her mother going to be well and strong again?

Sylvia kept her worries hidden, a silent cry of fear and pain nestled close to her heart, as she and her parents dressed for the cold and carried the baskets outside to the car. Her father rarely drove anymore, conserving the expensive gasoline for emergencies. Sylvia's mother had been told that her husband preferred to exercise the horses rather than allow them to grow fat and lazy over the winter. As far as Sylvia knew, her mother had accepted this, even though it was not what the Bergstroms had always done. They did so many things differently now, and yet nothing had raised the suspicions of the woman who had always known the intimate details of the household, who had known things about her children she could not possibly have seen or heard. How could she be so unaware of what was going on around her? Suddenly Sylvia was seized by the longing to take her mother by the shoulders and shake her, shake the truth into her and out of her.

Sylvia climbed into the backseat with the baskets while her father helped her mother into the front. The car coughed out a puff of black smoke from the tailpipe when her father tried to start it, but after a moment, the motor rumbled steadily.

"The Craigmiles first," Eleanor said. Her father nodded and drove them to a farm less than a mile away. The Craigmiles had lived in the Elm Creek Valley for generations, and their family had been friends with the Bergstroms since Gerda's time.

Sylvia's father waited in the car while his wife and daughter went up to the house; Sylvia carried the strudel, and her mother rested a hand on her shoulder for support. When Mrs. Craigmile opened the door to Eleanor's knock, Sylvia could tell her mother was taken aback by how much she had changed. Though she was only ten years older than Eleanor, her dark brown hair had gone gray, and deep crevices of worry framed her eyes and mouth.

Eleanor swiftly composed herself. "Merry Christmas, Edith." She nodded to Sylvia, who placed a wrapped strudel in her neighbor's hands.

"Well, my goodness." Mrs. Craigmile stared at the gift. "Thank you. I'm grateful. We weren't expecting anything, not this year."

"Why not?" said Eleanor, clearly surprised. "You must know we'd never forget you."

"Yes, but this year . . ." Mrs. Craigmile shrugged. "Hard times have hit everyone. But you're looking well. It's good to see you're getting out of the house."

"I do shut myself indoors too much as soon as the weather turns colder. It must be my city constitution."

Mrs. Craigmile's lips curved in an unsteady smile. "You've lived among us so long you surely must be accustomed to our climate by now. I've never lived anywhere but here. I can't imagine what I'll do if we have to clear out."

"You want to give up your farm?"

"Want to? It's not even our farm, or so we're told. It's the bank's."

Eleanor gripped Sylvia's shoulder tighter. "But Craigmiles have worked this land for more than a hundred years. What does the bank have to do with it?"

"Remember when the Brennans put those fifteen acres along our north pasture up for sale?"

"Of course. You and Malcolm purchased them."

"Times were better then. We took out a loan from the Bank of Waterford to buy the land, and add that summer porch to the house, and get that new tiller." Mrs. Craigmile shrugged matter-of-factly, but her grief was palpable. "When the bank failed, they called in our debt. Now some bankers in Philadelphia say they own the land. I don't know whether we should pack up and leave with all we can carry before they take the clothes off our backs, or if we should do as Malcolm says and stay put until they force us off."

The shock on Eleanor's face made Sylvia sick to her stomach. Mrs. Craigmile must have sensed something amiss, for she hastily added, "But don't you worry about us. We'll be fine. What would a bunch of city bankers want with our farm? They're likely to leave us be, especially if we promise to send them a little something every month. We'll get by. You folks have a good Christmas, you hear?"

Eleanor nodded wordlessly. Sylvia

breathed a quick Merry Christmas and accompanied her mother back to the waiting car.

"Did you know about the bank failure, Sylvia?" her mother asked.

"Yes, Mama," she replied in a small voice.

Her mother nodded, her eyes fixed on the car.

As they climbed into their seats, Sylvia held her breath, waiting for her mother to confront her father, to demand an accounting of their own circumstances. But she said nothing except to ask him to drive them on to the Shropshire farm, closer to town.

At every house they visited that morning it was the same. Friends and neighbors welcomed Eleanor and her gifts more gratefully than ever, inquired circumspectly after her health and the Bergstroms' prospects, and shared stories of misfortune that they clearly assumed Eleanor already knew. In town it was the same as on the farms. A schoolteacher said that half her pupils had dropped off the rolls. The wife of the editor of the *Waterford Register* confessed that she did not know how much longer her husband would be able to keep the paper going, and it would take all she had to scrape together a decent Christmas for the children. "But Santa won't forget them," she added, glancing at Sylvia as if noticing her for the first time. "Nor will he forget you."

She looked questioningly at Eleanor before adding the last. Whatever her silent question was, Sylvia's mother affirmed it with a quick nod and said, "I'm sure Santa will put in an appearance at our home tonight."

After the last strudel was delivered, Sylvia's father turned the car toward home. Throughout the trip, Eleanor had remained mostly silent. Sylvia's father had glanced at her now and then to be sure she was all right, and no doubt he attributed her silence to fatigue. Sylvia wanted to warn him that her mother knew the secrets he had kept so well for so long, but she did not see how to do it without betraying her mother.

As they crossed the bridge over Elm Creek, Eleanor suddenly broke the silence. "Freddy," she said quietly, "our neighbors are suffering."

Sylvia's father said nothing for a long moment. "Of course they are. These are hard times for everyone."

"And I had no idea how hard until today.

Oh, I knew our circumstances had to be worse than you were telling me, but I never conceived of anything so grim."

"Darling, I promise you we will manage. We won't lose the farm. The children won't starve."

"Perhaps, but what of our friends? What of the others? We must help them." Eleanor turned in her seat until she faced her husband. "The Craigmiles will lose their farm to the bank unless they pay off the loan. We must pay it for them."

"Darling —"

"Daniel Shropshire needs glasses. The Schultzes need food. No one has been able to pay Dr. Granger for months, so even his family is struggling. We must give more than simply the hope and joy of the season this year. We must give them what they need."

"Darling, we haven't the means."

Eleanor stared at him. "Then the bank failure —"

"Took our savings as well. Eleanor, as much as I long to help our friends, I'm doing all I can to keep our own heads above water."

Sylvia shrank back into her seat, sick at heart, wishing she were as deaf to their words as her parents seemed to believe.

Her mother sat straight up in her seat, gloved hands clasped in her lap, as her father pulled the car into the old carriage house and shut it down. No one moved to leave the car, and at last Sylvia's mother said, "As Christians we are not called to give from our surplus but to give all we can. We must sell the horses."

"Eleanor." Her father's voice was full of compassion and pain. "I haven't been able to sell a horse in months. Believe me, I've tried."

"But our most loyal customers —"

"— are broke, or in the same shape we are. It's the same everywhere. We all have to weather this storm together."

"Yes. You're absolutely right." Eleanor opened the car door, climbed out, and slammed it shut. "Together. That is the only way we will endure. We can't think only of ourselves. And you mustn't hide the truth from me ever again."

Sylvia's father watched her stride briskly toward the house. Sylvia sat perfectly still, her heart pounding. She had never witnessed such a heated exchange between her parents, and it was a thing both terrible and exhilarating. *Look!* she wanted to shout to her father and the aunts, *Mama is not too sick for the truth. She is strong and angry and determined. She will prove all of you wrong and make everything better, including herself.*

"Come along, Sylvia," said her father tiredly. "Let's get inside before we freeze."

Inside, they found the rest of the family unpacking Christmas ornaments and teasing Uncle William and Aunt Nellie as they dressed for a snowy walk through the woods in search of a Christmas tree. Sylvia's mother, Claudia reported, had briefly wished the couple well before heading upstairs to rest, or so everyone assumed. Sylvia joined in the decorating with a heavy heart. She wondered if anyone else noticed how often her father glanced to the doorway, how forced his smiles were.

The couple returned with a tree after little more than an hour had passed, earning them raised eyebrows and speculative looks instead of the thanks Sylvia thought they deserved for making up for the previous year by returning so promptly.

"Should we get Mama?" Claudia asked Sylvia as their father and uncle set the tree into its stand. "She wouldn't want to miss decorating the tree."

"I'll get her," said Sylvia. She slipped from the ballroom before her father could see her. He would not want her to disturb her mother.

Sylvia hurried upstairs to her mother's room, expecting to find her in bed, but instead discovering her seated on the floor taking clothes from a bureau drawer. Beside her was a pile of sweaters, neatly folded.

"Mama?" asked Sylvia. "What are you doing?"

"Sylvia, darling." Eleanor motioned for Sylvia to come to her. "I'm gathering clothes I no longer need. We'll take them to church tomorrow and ask Reverend Webster to distribute them to people in need."

Sylvia eyed the pile of sweaters. They were sturdy and warm, the kind her mother had worn when she helped exercise the horses. "Won't you need them?"

Eleanor shook her head. "They're too big for me now." And it was true; over the years her mother had grown thinner, a willow swaying in the wind. "I would like you to go to your closet and take out any dresses you've outgrown. Shoes, too. I'm sure the reverend can find a young lady who will be glad to have them."

"Now, Mama? Everyone is downstairs trimming the tree."

Eleanor started. "Oh, my goodness, of course they are. We mustn't keep them waiting. We can finish this tomorrow."

Spend Christmas Day sorting old clothes? Sylvia was about to protest, but the stories their neighbors had told of hard times and harder yet on the horizon tugged at her and she fell silent. She took her mother's hand and accompanied her downstairs. They passed Great-Aunt Lydia, sent out to hide the star. She seemed happily surprised to see Eleanor, and she teased Sylvia in passing about searching for the star before it was properly hidden. Ordinarily a remark like that would have left Sylvia feeling indignant and wrongfully accused, but too many other more upsetting things had been said that day for a harmless joke to trouble her.

When they entered the ballroom, Sylvia's father hurried over, took his wife's hands, and led her to a comfortable chair where she could observe the decorating and offer suggestions. Sylvia half expected her mother to argue that she did not need to sit, but Eleanor took the seat offered her and asked Sylvia to fetch her sewing. Sylvia ran to the parlor for the sewing basket and holly appliqués, and not long after she returned, her father sent the children out to find the red glass star. Sylvia remembered where Great-Aunt Lydia had hidden the star the last time she had taken a turn, three years before. Eager to return to her mother, Sylvia looked there first and discovered the star on a bookshelf in the library, though not the same bookshelf. Sylvia took Richard by the hand and guided him to it; he crowed with joy and raced back to show his parents what he had found.

And so Christmas Eve passed as all those in Sylvia's memory had passed, or nearly so. Great-Aunt Lucinda read aloud Christmas greetings from distant family, including cousin Elizabeth's letter from California. Sylvia's father read "A Visit from St. Nicholas" aloud to the children, and Great-Aunt Lydia followed with the story of the Nativity from St. Luke. Sylvia's mother sewed holly berry appliqués to her Christmas Quilt, and Great-Aunt Lucinda passed around a plate of her Christmas cookies. But there were fewer cookies than last year, and fewer presents beneath the tree. Sylvia hoped Santa would not forget that most of those were gifts the adults would exchange, and that there was room beneath the tree for more for the children.

The children were sent off to bed with hugs and kisses. Sylvia led toddler Richard by the hand and tucked him into bed, as she did every night. When she went to her own room, Claudia was already under the covers. "What happened when you and Mama and Daddy went out this morning?" Claudia asked as Sylvia climbed into bed.

"We took strudel to the neighbors, just like always."

"But you were gone so long."

"Mama made more strudel this year."

"She might think this will be the last year for it."

Sylvia felt a thundering in her skull as the nagging suspicion she had tried to ignore all day erupted to the surface. It was true. Each giving that day had been an expression of friendship, of sympathy during hard times, of the joy and hope of the season — but also of farewell.

Musing, Claudia added, "It's almost as if Mama thinks we'll always be this poor, that we'll never have enough flour to bake properly again."

Gratefully, desperately, Sylvia seized on to her sister's innocent explanation and held fast. Of course their mother's gifts were linked to the hard times in Waterford. Of course she would want to give out as many strudel as possible to make sure their friends had a special breakfast Christmas morning. From what Mrs. Craigmile and the others had said, even the most ordinary meals of the past had come to seem luxurious. Their mother's gifts would remind their friends that better times were sure to come again. She was offering them hope and encouragement with every bite of delicate pastry and cinnamon apples.

"We aren't poor." Sylvia pulled the quilt up to her chin. "We're a lot better off than most people, especially the families who live in town. We'll always get by as long as we have the farm."

"That's true. Daddy can always sell some of the land."

"That's not what I meant. We have the farm and the orchards and our home. We'll never starve and we'll always have a roof over our heads. That's all we need."

"Everyone needs money, even if they own a farm. We have to pay taxes and buy the things we can't make or grow." Claudia spread her glossy brown curls in a fan on her pillow to keep her hair free of snarls, as she did every night. She slept on her back and in the morning her hair would still be spread out obediently, without the smallest tangle. Sylvia could never figure out how

Claudia managed to keep still all night, while Sylvia always woke tangled in the bed sheets.

"I don't mean sell all of the land," Claudia added. "We would never sell the manor and leave us without a home. But Daddy will sell the land if he has to. I know I would."

Anger stirred within Sylvia. "It's a good thing Elm Creek Manor will never be yours to sell."

She rolled over on her side and folded her pillow around her head, her back to her sister. Claudia was a fool, a silly little fool. The farm sustained their family. The land took care of the Bergstroms as much as they took care of the land. Their father knew this. Every Bergstrom with an ounce of sense understood that implicitly, just as they understood the necessity of air to breathe and food to eat. How Claudia could so blithely contemplate selling off Bergstrom land filled Sylvia with equal parts astonishment and anger.

Christmas morning dawned gray and cold. Snow had fallen overnight, and the dense clouds gave a twilight cast to the morning air, but the weather had not prevented Santa from coming. Sylvia forgot her frustration with her sister and her worries about their neighbors in the particular happiness that was Christmas morning. Santa had come. He had forgiven her the innumerable acts of naughtiness she had committed throughout the year and had placed her on his good list, a surer sign of his love and his faith in her potential than an accurate evaluation of her behavior. She could even be happy for Claudia, who had received the china doll she had longed for. Little Richard had found a wooden train beneath the tree and was happily pushing it around in circles on the floor. Sylvia received a sewing basket of her very own, exactly like her mother's except for the color — a cheerful pine instead of dark cherry wood.

"Santa must have seen you helping me with the Christmas Quilt," her mother remarked. "He must have decided you needed scissors and needles of your own."

Sylvia would have been content with that one gift, but just then her father peered curiously into the branches of the tree. "What's that?" he asked, gesturing.

"I don't see anything," said Claudia, "just a bit of paper. Maybe it fell from Sylvia's angel. The wings have always been loose. She didn't use enough paste."

Sylvia glared at Claudia before remembering that Santa might already be watching and taking notes for next year.

Her father shook his head, puzzled. "It's a bit of paper, all right, but look up to the higher branches. The wings of Sylvia's angel are right where they belong. Sylvia, will you see what it is?"

Sylvia closed her sewing basket and set it aside. She rose on tiptoe and reached into the tree where a small bit of white was visible through the branches and needles. It was a piece of heavy writing paper, folded over and sealed with a spot of red wax. Her own name was written in fancy script upon it.

"It's a letter, I think," she said. "To me."

"A letter?" Sylvia's mother glanced at her father, surprised. "Who is it from?"

"Santa?" joked Uncle William.

"Who else would have left a surprise in our Christmas tree?" said Sylvia's father. "Read it aloud, Sylvia. Tell us what old St. Nick has to say for himself."

Quickly Sylvia broke the seal and unfolded the paper. " 'Dear Sylvia,' " she read. " 'I hope you like the sewing basket I left for you. I trust you weren't too disappointed that I could not bring you all the toys you wanted. I'm sure you know that folks have fallen on hard times in your part of the world. This year I had to fill up my sleigh with food and clothes as well as toys for all those good little children who don't have warm homes and plenty to eat, like you and your sister and brother do. Unfortunately, my sleigh was too heavy for my reindeer to pull, so I had to leave a few bags of toys back at the North Pole. I will do my best to bring them next year, but you're such a generous, kind little girl that I know you'll understand.'"

"He can't be talking about Sylvia," interrupted Claudia. "I think he put her name on there by mistake."

"Claudia," admonished their mother.

Sylvia ignored her sister and read on. " 'I know you won't miss those toys when you find out what a special present I've planned for you to receive soon. I couldn't bring it on my sleigh and it wouldn't fit under the tree. I know you'll take very good care of it because you're so helpful to your mother and your great-aunts, and because you take such loving care of your little brother.' "

"Now I know he got our names mixed up," declared Claudia.

"Claudia, hush," said their father.

"What present wouldn't fit under a tree?" asked Uncle William, scratching his head. "What's that jolly old elf talking about? Maybe he's been sipping too much eggnog."

Claudia giggled, but Sylvia kept reading. " 'I'm sure you know Blossom is due to have her foal soon. You tell your father that I said you get to have that foal for your very own horse.' " Sylvia stopped reading and looked up at her father.

"Go on," her mother prompted. "This has suddenly become quite interesting."

"I'll say," said Uncle William.

Sylvia took a deep breath and plunged ahead. " 'I know you'll take very good care of your horse and that you will make me very proud. Until next year, I remain very truly yours, Santa Claus. P.S.: Merry Christmas!' " She gulped and looked from her mother to her father. "Can he do that? Can he make you give me one of the horses for my very own?"

Her father shrugged. "Who am I to argue with Santa Claus? If he thinks you're ready to join the family business, I'm going to trust his judgment."

"Why is Sylvia the only one who gets a horse?" protested Claudia.

Their mother turned to her. "Why, Claudia, do you want a horse?"

Claudia's mouth worked in a scowl.

"No," she grumbled.

"Santa probably knows you're scared of horses," reasoned Sylvia. "And you got the doll and all those clothes. And Richard's too little to take care of a horse. So it's just me. Daddy, can we go see Blossom right now?"

"After breakfast," her father promised.

Sylvia had almost forgotten that breakfast would include the strudel she and Claudia had helped her mother make. She knew it was the same one because she had pinched an edge of the pastry just so, wanting to be sure she would recognize it later. To her relief, it was as flavorful and flaky as those her grandmother had made. Everyone around the table said so.

After breakfast, Sylvia went with her father and uncle to the stables. She greeted Blossom gently, fed her a special Christmas treat of oats and apples, and promised always to take very good care of her little foal.

The snow fell heavily throughout the day, keeping away visitors who had not arrived on Christmas Eve. It was a smaller, quieter Christmas than in years past, and the older members of the family spoke wistfully of loved ones who had passed on, how they would have admired the tree, enjoyed the girls' first strudel, and marveled at the letter from Santa Claus. Later that day, Sylvia's mother sent the girls off to collect clothing and toys in good repair to give to the less fortunate. This became another Bergstrom tradition, and when prosperity returned, their gifts became more generous — new clothes and toys instead of old, sacks of groceries for the food pantry, checks to the soup kitchen the students of Waterford College established near campus. In years to come, Sylvia was pleased to think that so much had come from her mother's compassionate insistence that they must give more than what they thought they could afford, and if they did, they would surprise themselves with the unsuspected depths of their good fortune.

A few months later, when Blossom's foal was born, Sylvia named her Dresden Rose after one of her mother's favorite quilt blocks. The gentle horse provided Sylvia with the comfort of a loyal friend as her mother's health waned. A day arrived when Eleanor no longer had the strength to come downstairs to the parlor to sit and quilt and fondly watch over her children. Then she no longer left her bedroom at all.

Once, in the night, Sylvia heard her

mother weeping. She stole from bed and listened at her parents' door, and as she listened she learned that her mother wept not because she could not bear the physical pain, but because she did not believe she would live to see her children grow up. What grieved her most of all was that Richard was so young, he was not likely to remember her, to remember how dearly she had loved him.

For once, Sylvia regretted eavesdropping on her elders. She crept back to bed and cried into her pillow until she fell asleep.

Eleanor Bergstrom died before the end of summer. She was laid to rest in the Bergstrom plot of their church's small cemetery. Her father dug up a lilac bush from Eleanor's favorite place on the estate and replanted it near her grave, so that in springtime she would once again be near the fragrant blossoms that had brought her so much pleasure.

The first Christmas of what came to be known as the Great Depression was Eleanor's last. For Sylvia, no Christmas that followed was ever as joyful or as blessed as those that lived on in her memory, when her family was whole, when she was a child loved by a mother.

"If I could have just one more day with

my mother," said Sylvia. "Just one more day to quilt with her, to taste the meals she prepared with such love, to tell her — oh, I would have so much to tell her. And your mother is just a few hours' drive away, and you cannot even pick up the phone and invite her to come for Christmas. I tell you, Sarah, someday you are going to regret not making that call."

Sarah gaped at her, her hand frozen in the act of shelving a box of dehydrated potatoes in the pantry. "I'll call her," she said when she found her voice. "If I had known how much it meant to you, I would have done it earlier."

"Don't do it for my sake but for your own," said Sylvia, an ache of longing catching in her throat.

Chapter Three

Sylvia left Sarah alone in the kitchen. On her way out, she passed Matt carrying the CD player back to the kitchen. "Tell Sarah not to disappoint me," she told him firmly. She would leave it up to Sarah whether to explain what she meant.

Sylvia crossed the marble foyer, still gaily strewn with Christmas decorations, and climbed the grand oak staircase to her bedroom on the second floor. If Carol accepted her daughter's invitation — and why would she not? — they would need to finish decking the manor's halls at record speed. Now Sylvia regretted her earlier strategic interference in Sarah's decorating, and she had half a mind to hurry back downstairs and send the young couple out for a tree that minute — but rather than risk interrupting Sarah's phone call, she would wait.

They would have a tree up soon enough, and it would be fitting to have a present for Carol beneath it. Sarah and Matt had likely mailed her gifts already. Carol would not be expecting anything else, and certainly, the hope and joy of the season manifest in her daughter's invitation would be gift enough. But even so, Sylvia would like to give Carol something herself. She had recently finished a blue-and-white Hunter's Star quilt that she had intended to sell on commission at Grandma's Attic, Waterford's only quilt shop; it would make a lovely gift. If Sarah kept to her promise to call her mother, with any luck, Carol would be there to unwrap it Christmas morning.

Sylvia found a box for the Hunter's Star quilt and wrapped it in cheerful red-and-white striped paper, and then attended to Sarah and Matt's gifts. For Matt she had purchased a set of gardener's tools he had admired in a catalog; for Sarah, she had chosen a wheeled art cart with three drawers full of notions and gadgets guaranteed to thrill the heart of any quilter. Matt had helped her assemble it, but Sylvia had packed the drawers herself, arranging the acrylic rulers and rotary cutters just so. It was no mean feat to wrap the contraption, and after some early thwarted attempts to conceal the entire cart, she decided to cover only the sides and the top and to leave the wheeled underside alone. Sarah would not mind.

Sylvia was nearly finished when she heard the phone ring down the hall in the library. *Carol,* she thought. She must have been away from the phone when Sarah called and was returning her message. Sylvia continued wrapping gifts, allowing Sarah the opportunity to answer. But the ringing continued uninterrupted until it was abruptly silenced when the answering machine picked up. "Oh, for heaven's sake," grumbled Sylvia, hurrying to the library while the outgoing message played. She snatched up the phone just before the beep. "Good morning. Elm Creek Quilts."

"Good morning, Sylvia." The caller's voice was difficult to make out over the background of children's shrieks and laughter. "It's Agnes."

"Why, hello, dear." Sylvia sat down behind the large oak desk. "It sounds like you have a houseful."

"That's an understatement. I don't know who's causing more commotion, the five grandchildren or the four parents trying to settle them down."

"At least with you there the children don't have the adults outnumbered." Sylvia winced at the sound of glass shattering. "What was that?"

"Nothing, just a bowl." Agnes's voice became muffled, as if she had covered the mouthpiece. "Sweetie, stay off the kitchen floor until Grandma cleans that up. You have bare feet."

"Is there anything I can do? Do you need some spare quilts or pillows? Or perhaps a rescue squad?"

"No, we're all fine here. A little cramped, but we'll manage. I'd rather be crowded than alone on Christmas, wouldn't you?"

"That depends," said Sylvia. She would be happier alone if it meant Sarah was en route to her mother's.

"Oh, Sylvia. I don't buy that for a minute. Even you want company at Christmas. Which brings me to the point. Are you going to be home later this afternoon? I wanted to stop by and wish you a Merry Christmas in person."

Sylvia smiled at her sister-in-law's poorly disguised hint that she wanted to drop off Sylvia's Christmas present. "I don't have any plans to go out. Stop by anytime. Bring the grandkids."

"Thanks, but we're trying to contain this hurricane. It will just be me and one of my girls."

They made plans for her visit, and Sylvia hung up the phone, disappointed. Her invitation to the children was sincere, as much for herself as for Agnes. She missed the sounds of children playing in Elm Creek Manor, running through the halls and thundering up and down the stairs the way she and her siblings and cousins had done.

Perhaps next year.

Sylvia returned to her room. After wrapping her gifts and fixing the bows and tags in place, Sylvia went downstairs to the foyer, where the decorating had apparently made little progress since the last time she had passed through. Perhaps, she thought hopefully, Sarah was finally on the phone with her mother, making arrangements for her visit, offering driving directions, assuring her she did not need to bring anything for Christmas dinner the next day. Smiling, Sylvia found herself humming carols as she unpacked a box of red velvet ribbons of varying widths. She and Claudia had used them to tie up boughs of greenery they gathered from the strand of pines beyond the orchard. Perhaps she could send Matthew out to cut some before he and Sarah went searching for a tree. The Bergstroms had loved to put evergreen branches throughout the manor — on fireplace mantels, above mirrors and picture frames, everywhere that a touch of green and the scent of pine would make a room more festive. Claudia had liked to set candles among them; the effect was lovely, especially on a snowy night.

Sylvia added a few last touches to the foyer and decided that fresh greenery was all she needed to make the room complete. She went to the front parlor and rapped softly on the door before entering, but Sarah was not on the phone. Sylvia headed for the kitchen, quickening her pace. It was not necessarily a bad sign that the phone call had ended so soon. Perhaps they had needed only a few minutes to make Carol's arrangements.

From the hallway outside the kitchen, Sylvia heard the familiar clatter of a sewing machine. Frowning, she strode into the west sitting room and discovered Sarah bent over Sylvia's Featherweight sewing machine, stitching Eleanor's holly sprays to a row of Lucinda's Feathered Stars. Matthew was nowhere to be seen.

"What do you think you're doing?" exclaimed Sylvia.

Sarah looked up, startled. "I'm working on the Christmas Quilt. What's wrong?

Did you want me to sew by hand instead?"

"What I wanted was for you to call your mother."

"I did call her," said Sarah, indignant. "I told you I would, and I did."

"And?"

"And we talked. She received the gifts Matt and I sent. The sweater fits but she doesn't like the color, so she's going to exchange it."

Exasperated, Sylvia nearly shouted, "Is she coming to visit or isn't she?"

"No." Sarah busied herself with pinning a seam. "She thanked you for the invitation, but she had already made other plans. The neighbors across the street invited her to celebrate with their family. They always have a big crowd, and my mom's known them for years. She'll have a good time."

Sylvia raised a hand to her brow and sighed, defeated. If only she had thought to ask Sarah to invite her mother weeks ago. Next year, she would remember. Or better yet, she would ask Carol and make all the arrangements herself. Sarah needn't know of it until her mother walked through the front door, suitcase in hand. Let Sarah try to wriggle out of talking to her mother then!

Sarah studied her, curious. "Just this

morning you insisted you wanted a quiet Christmas all alone, and now you're the picture of despair because my mother turned down a last-minute invitation. I don't get it, Sylvia."

Wasn't it obvious? All Sylvia wanted for Christmas was a peaceful exchange between two stubborn women, a few cautious but determined steps toward reconciliation. Carol had reached out by inviting Sarah home, but Sarah had rebuffed her, and now she seemed relieved — cheerful, even — that her mother was not coming.

"At least you tried," said Sylvia, doubting her young friend had extended the invitation graciously. "Maybe next year."

"No, next year it's Matt's father's turn."

"But you skipped your mother's turn."

"No, *she* skipped it. She doesn't get a do-over."

"My goodness, Sarah, this is your relationship with your mother we're talking about, not a game of Parcheesi. No wonder your mother declined, if you invited her this grudgingly."

Sarah's cheeks flushed. "If you knew the whole story, you wouldn't side with my mother. If you could see for yourself how she treats Matt, you'd understand why I don't want to force him to endure her company."

"It can't be as bad as all that."

"You're right. It's worse. Matt is a wonderful man and he loves me, but my mother thinks I've married beneath myself because he's not some white collar professional. She refuses to believe he's anything more than a maintenance man. And even if he were, what's wrong with that? Having a blue collar job doesn't make you a bad husband any more than working in an office cubicle guarantees you'll be a good one."

Though her loyalties were to Sarah and Matt, Sylvia tried to look at the situation from Carol's point of view. Sarah and Matt had met as students at Penn State, where Sarah earned a bachelor's degree in accounting and Matt in landscape architecture. Upon graduating, Sarah found a position as a cost accountant for a local convenience store chain in State College, while Matt was promoted to a full-time position from his former part-time job working on the Penn State campus. Unfortunately, Matt lost his job when the state legislature slashed the university's budget, and when his search for another position in State College proved fruitless, he looked farther afield, to Waterford. In agreeing to the move for Matt's sake, Sarah had admittedly taken a risk in sacrificing her secure position and steady income, but it was a tedious and uninspiring job, and she had been glad to be free of it. Their gamble had paid off in a multitude of ways, but parents tended to be cautious where their children were concerned, and perhaps Sarah and Matt had taken too many risks with their careers for Carol's taste.

Sylvia tried to shed a positive light on Carol's concerns. "She probably only needs reassurance that he will be a good provider. Many parents believe that no one is good enough to marry their children."

"I'm not going to forward copies of his pay stubs just to appease her," Sarah declared. "It wouldn't help anyway. She's so convinced he'll never amount to anything that she twists his every achievement into a sign of his imminent failure. When he received his degree at Penn State, she started calling him 'that gardener.' When he accepted the job that brought us to Waterford, she carried on about how he was dragging me off to the middle of nowhere and ruining my career. When he switched jobs to work as your caretaker, she sent me a three-page letter warning me about the dangers of allowing our incomes to be dependent upon the whims of an old woman."

Sylvia sucked in a breath. "She said that?"

"And much more, from the day I first told her we were dating. Sylvia, I know you think I've stayed away out of petulance or spite, but that's not it. I can't forgive my mother for the cruel things she's said about the man I love, and I'm keeping them apart so she can't hurt him." Sarah frowned and fingered one of the Feathered Stars. "Until she can promise to treat my husband with respect, I don't want to share the same room with her."

Sylvia sat down heavily on her chair — then rose quickly and moved the forgotten book to the side table. "I had no idea it was as bad as all that. I thought you were —"

"Exaggerating?"

Sylvia nodded.

Sarah let out a short laugh, empty of humor. "I knew it. Believe me, the opposite is true. I could tell you stories — Okay. Here's one, just to give you a taste. Matt and I had been married for about two years when we spent Christmas with my mother for the first time. Do you know what she had under the tree? Season tickets to the Pittsburgh Steelers for her then-boyfriend, a gorgeous Italian leather briefcase for me, and do you know what she had for Matt?"

Sylvia muffled a sigh. "I dare not hazard a guess."

"A fruitcake."

"You can't expect me to believe that."

"It's true! A fruitcake in a tin shaped like Santa's workshop."

"Well —" Sylvia struggled for a positive interpretation. "Why not? It's a holiday favorite. I bet it was a very good fruitcake."

"That's a bet you would lose. It was the exact same fruitcake she had received as a gift from the hospital board of directors five years before. All of the nurses get something from the same mail order company each year. She probably thought I forgot, but I didn't."

"It seems odd that she would save a fruitcake so long," said Sylvia. "How can you be certain she didn't buy it for Matt that year because the one she had received from the hospital was so delicious?"

Sarah gave her a look that said, *because I'm not stupid.* "It came sealed in plastic with a very visible 'Use Before' date stamped on it."

"Oh, dear."

"I was so proud of Matt. He thanked my mom and actually looked pleased that she had given him something. I think maybe he really was."

"Well," said Sylvia weakly, "it is the thought that counts."

"Exactly! What was she thinking, giving him stale fruitcake? It wasn't even edible. Compare that to the expensive gifts she bought for me and her then-boyfriend. It would have been better if she had given us nothing."

"Well —" Sylvia did not know how to defend Carol, and she was no longer sure she wanted to. "I imagine you confronted your mother."

"Not really. I merely trapped her in her own deceit. On Christmas Day, with all the relatives present, I suggested that we serve the fruitcake with coffee for dessert. I took it into the kitchen and sawed off a few slices and set them on a nice serving plate. My mother hovered over me the entire time making a fuss about how she had already made a pecan pie and she didn't want it to go to waste and how I really should have let Matt take the fruitcake home. Later, when her then-boyfriend took a piece from the buffet, she swooped in and snatched his plate before he could break a tooth. Fortunately, no one else took a piece or she would have been grabbing plates left and right for the rest of the day. I don't know what happened to the tin. Before we left the next morning, I asked my mother for it, saying that I wanted to use it to store Christmas cards. She said it was in the dishwasher but she couldn't open the door in the middle of the cycle, so she would mail it to us. Of course she never did."

"Perhaps it was lost in the mail."

"Oh, sure. That's fair. When in doubt, blame it on the hardworking postal service instead of my malicious mother."

Sylvia was at a loss. "How does Matt feel about all this?"

"You know him, the eternal optimist. He still believes that once my mother has a chance to get to know him, she'll accept him. I'm a realist. I know it would take a miracle for that to happen."

"Christmas is a time for miracles."

"This would take a miracle on the order of the parting of the Red Sea, and I'm not holding my breath." Sarah shook her head and slid fabric beneath the presser foot of the sewing machine. "See, Sylvia, your family has its Christmas traditions: German cookies and decorating a tree in the ballroom. My family has ours: using Christmas gifts to express our spite and taking extra early-morning shifts so we can avoid our family. Maybe now you can understand why I'd rather stay here."

The bitterness in her young friend's voice pained Sylvia. Her mother had acted with appalling rudeness, but even so, Sylvia could not help marveling at the pettiness of it all. To harbor such anger and resentment over a Christmas gift! Sylvia regretted that Carol Mallory had been so unkind to steadfast, good-natured Matt, but she could not condone Sarah's decision to keep the two apart because of it. She rather agreed with Matt. Surely if Carol had more opportunity to discover what a fine young man he was, her disapproval would lessen until it eventually ceased.

Sylvia sat pondering while Sarah worked on the Christmas Quilt, ruefully aware that her plan to bring together Sarah and her mother had been doomed from the beginning. Their relationship was clearly in worse shape than Sylvia had realized, and no thrown-together Christmas reunion would rectify things. Christmas was the season of peace, but somehow people often forgot to include the harmony of their own family in their prayers for peace on earth and goodwill toward all. The stress and excitement of the holidays often laid bare the hairline cracks in the facade of ostensibly functional families. No wonder Sarah preferred to work on another family's abandoned quilt than on her own family's unresolved disagreements.

Sarah did seem to be making remarkable progress on the quilt, although Sylvia was not quite certain how she intended for those very dissimilar blocks to come together harmoniously. She had attached border sashing to some of Lucinda's Feathered Stars and joined four together in pairs. With a few added seams, Eleanor's holly sprays had been transformed into open plumes, which Sarah was in the midst of attaching to Claudia's Variable Stars.

"That's a sure way to ruin it," muttered Sylvia. Louder, over the cheerful clatter of the sewing machine, she added, "Sarah, dear, I thought I told you not to bother including Claudia's blocks in the quilt."

Amused, Sarah said, "You suggested that I could leave them out if I thought they would ruin the quilt, and I told you that I wouldn't dream of leaving her out of a family quilt. I measured, and you're right; her blocks vary in size almost a half-inch, but my layout will account for that."

"But they're so plain and simple," protested Sylvia. "They aren't as intricate as the blocks my mother and great-aunt made."

"That's precisely why they work so well." Sarah continued sewing, completely indifferent to Sylvia's consternation. "Sometimes a simple block is needed to set off more elaborate designs. You taught me that."

Sylvia had always suspected that someday her preaching would come back to haunt her. "This is a very special quilt. You shouldn't include a block of inferior quality for sentimental reasons."

"A quilt, like a family, doesn't have to be perfect, but it does have to be inclusive."

"That's a remarkable philosophy from someone who refuses to give her mother a second chance to truly get to know her son-in-law."

"Said the woman who held a grudge against her sister for fifty years."

Sylvia had no reply.

"I'm sorry," said Sarah quickly. "I know what happened between you two was much more than a grudge. I didn't mean to make light of it."

But Sylvia knew Sarah was not entirely

wrong. "Think nothing of it. We've exchanged strong words before and survived."

Sarah searched her face for a moment to be sure Sylvia was not angry, frowned briefly in uncertainty, and returned to her work with an almost imperceptible shake of the head.

Sylvia watched as the hapless Variable Star blocks were joined with her mother's exquisite appliqué and knew that somewhere, Claudia was laughing.

Sylvia had once overheard her father say that she had come into the world looking for a fight, and as the Bergstrom closest to her in age, Claudia had quickly become her unwitting rival. Sylvia, naturally, saw the situation differently. It was Claudia who was constantly competing with her, Claudia who sparked the arguments and stirred up animosity and yet somehow always managed to appear blameless to the adults of the family.

Even as a child Sylvia understood why adults preferred Claudia. She was such an obvious favorite that Sylvia almost did not blame them for it. Claudia was two years older, but since Sylvia was bright for her age and tall, everyone treated them as if they were the same age, and comparisons were unavoidable. Claudia was the beauty; she had been blessed with their mother's grace and the best features of the Bergstroms. The oldest members of the family declared that she was the very image of great-grandmother Anneke, a famous beauty of her day, but they respected their ancestors too much to hold any of them responsible for Sylvia's appearance, even though her remarkable height, strong chin, and assertive posture were unmistakably Bergstrom. Claudia's hair, the rich brown hue of maple sugar, hung down her back nearly to her waist in glossy waves, while Sylvia's, the color of the burnt bits scraped off toast, tended to be snarled and windblown from the time she spent outdoors hanging around the stables, pestering her father with pleas to be allowed to ride. Sylvia was the better student, mastering her lessons easily and impatient for more, but Claudia won the teachers' hearts with her obedience and charming manners. She never failed to be sweet and cheerful, even as she misspelled half the words in her themes. For her part, Sylvia was moody and sensitive, and she could not hide her resentment at being compared unfavorably to the lovely creature who had passed through that teacher's classroom two years before. For as long as Sylvia could remember, she had been convinced that she was a terrible disappointment to their mother, an inferior second effort after the overwhelming success that was her firstborn.

From an early age, each of the sisters had struggled to prove herself better than the other in every conceivable quality or activity. Sylvia won in academics, quilting, and innate ability with horses; Claudia, in everything else. Still, although Sylvia was best in what she considered the most important categories, her success was unsatisfying because Claudia seemed unaware of it. While Sylvia's report cards gave Claudia no alternative but to concede she was the better student, Claudia feared horses and did not care how well Sylvia rode or how docilely the strongest stallions responded to her attentions. She also would never admit, even when Sylvia confronted her with side-by-side comparisons of their stitches, that Sylvia was the more adept quilter. No matter how often Sylvia proved herself to be her sister's equal or better, Claudia refused to treat her as anything but a tag-along little sister, a nuisance, an afterthought.

Quilting — which for so many women and girls was an enjoyable, harmonious activity that encouraged friendship, sharing, and community — only sharpened their competitive natures. Their first quilting lesson with their mother turned into a race to see which girl could complete the most Nine-Patch blocks and win the right to sleep beneath the finished quilt first. When Sylvia gained an insurmountable lead, Claudia burst into tears, declared that she hated Sylvia, and ran from the room, scattering her meager pile of Nine-Patch blocks as she went. When Eleanor found out the reason for her outburst, she told Sylvia to apologize to her sister — which Sylvia did. "I'm sorry I sewed faster than you," she told Claudia, which outraged her sister and displeased all the grown-ups.

Sylvia ended up finishing that quilt alone. She gave it to a cousin, Uncle William and Aunt Nellie's four-year-old daughter, since Claudia would not allow it into their room.

A more sensible pair of girls would have avoided working together on a quilt again, but their second attempt came a year later, when their mother announced that she was expecting another child. Originally each girl had planned to sew her own quilt for the baby, but when they began to argue over which quilt their new brother or sister would use first, Eleanor decreed they would work together: Sylvia would choose the colors, Claudia the pattern, and each would sew precisely half of the blocks necessary for the top. It seemed like a reasonable plan, until Claudia did the unthinkable and chose the Turkey Tracks pattern. Not only was this a challenging block Sylvia doubted her sister could make well, but according to their grandmother, it also had a history of foreboding consequences. Once better known as the Wandering Foot, its name had been changed to divert the bad luck associated with it. Legend told that a boy given a Wandering Foot quilt would never be content to stay in one place, but would forever be restless, roaming the world, never settling down. A girl receiving such a quilt would be doomed to an even worse fate, so bleak that Grandmother refused to describe it. Eleanor and Claudia had heard Grandmother's warnings as often as Sylvia, but they laughed off Sylvia's concerns and told her not to be upset by silly superstitions. Defeated, all Sylvia could do was to select her lucky colors, blue and yellow, and hope that would be enough to offset the pattern's influence.

After their mother died, the fire went out of the girls' competitiveness around the quilting frame. Without their mother to impress, without a chance that she would finally admit a preference for the handiwork of one daughter over the other, there seemed no point to it.

Less than three years after losing their mother, Sylvia and Claudia decided to collaborate on a quilt once again, out of necessity rather than any anticipation of enjoyment. In January 1933, while browsing through a catalog from which their father often purchased farm tools, they learned about a marvelous quilt competition sponsored by Sears, Roebuck, and Company. If their quilt passed elimination rounds at their local store and at the regional level, it would be displayed in a special pavilion at the World's Fair in Chicago and be eligible for a $2,500 First Prize. Neither Sylvia nor Claudia had ever possessed such an enormous sum of money, and they were determined to enter.

In order to complete an entire masterpiece quilt by the May 15 deadline, they had no alternative but to work together. Claudia interpreted the rules to mean that each quilt must be the work of a single quilter, so she signed their entry form under the name "Claudia Sylvia Bergstrom," provoking Sylvia's ire when she discovered her billing had been reduced to her sister's middle name, or so everyone would believe. A more significant point of contention was the design of the quilt. Sylvia wanted to create an original pictorial quilt inspired by the World's Fair theme of "A Century of Progress," but Claudia thought the judges would be more impressed by a traditional pattern presented in flawless, intricate needlework. After wasting several weeks debating their design, they agreed to a compromise between tradition and novelty. Sylvia designed a central appliqué medallion depicting various scenes from Colonial times until the present day, which Claudia framed in a border of pieced blocks. To Sylvia's exasperation, Claudia selected the Odd Fellow's Chain pattern, squandering an opportunity to select a pattern with a more appropriately symbolic name. Sylvia did not complain, however, since it was a visually striking block her sister could handle more or less successfully, and it did inspire an intriguing title for their work: "Chain of Progress."

Despite their unpromising start, the sisters agreed on one point: "Chain of Progress" was the best quilt either had ever made. They took first place at the local competition in Harrisburg, but lost at the regional level in Philadelphia. Later that year, when their father took his three children by train to see the World's Fair, the sisters agreed on a second point: Their quilt was easily as lovely as any of the twenty-nine finalists displayed. Claudia was so disappointed by the loss of the admiration and status that would have accompanied a victory that Sylvia hadn't the heart to suggest that her uneven quilting stitches had probably cost them a place among the finalists.

Sylvia did not mind the loss as much as her sister. Though times were still hard and the Bergstroms had to watch every penny, their father had splurged on the trip to the World's Fair, reward enough for Sylvia. She also knew that, at age thirteen, she had many quilt competitions and blue ribbons in her future.

Time passed and other concerns left little room in her thoughts for mulling over her disappointment — namely, her younger brother Richard's progress in school. He was an apt pupil when it came to learning about horses — which pleased their father — but although he was bright, he had little patience for the classroom. Headstrong and mischievous, he dodged Sylvia's efforts to tutor him, and if she left him alone with a lesson to study, she would return later to find that he had run off to the barn, or the orchard, or more likely than not, the stables.

Sylvia blamed that Wandering Foot quilt.

In spite of his reluctance to study, he was clever enough to do well on his school work even when he only gave it half his attention. That, his kind heart, and his charm were his saving graces at school. He had light brown, wavy hair that brightened to gold in the summer, long-lashed, green-brown eyes that his sisters envied, and a dimple that appeared in his right cheek when he grinned, which was often. The teachers adored him and smiled when they called him a rascal, and he was popular among his classmates — not because he followed the crowd, but because he could usually persuade the crowd that his way of doing things was more fun.

In the autumn of the year after the Bergstroms' trip to the Chicago World's Fair, a new family moved into a ramshackle house on the outskirts of town. The parents and a young daughter were rarely seen, but their oldest child, a boy, attended the elementary school in Waterford. He was enrolled in Richard's class, and Sylvia often spotted him sitting alone by the fence when she and Claudia dropped off their brother on their way to their own school, a block away. She was appalled that any mother or father could send a child to school in such filthy clothes. His face was always peaked, weariness hung in his eyes, and his sleeves were often not long enough to cover the bruises on his arms.

Most of the schoolchildren shunned the newcomer, whose presence hinted at a darker world than the one they inhabited, one they might have sensed they themselves had escaped only by an accident of birth. Some of the bolder children teased him, but Richard put a stop to that. Sylvia observed the whole incident through the fence on the day Richard suddenly walked off the pitcher's mound and approached the boy as he watched from his usual spot by the fence. Richard asked the boy's name and invited him to join in the game. When the other boys protested, Richard said, "Okay, if you don't want Andrew on our team, him and me'll play catch instead."

"But you have the only ball," a boy in

the batter's box shouted. "We can't play without you."

Richard grinned and shrugged as if that had not occurred to him. "Then I guess you can't play without Andrew, either."

The loss of Richard's favor was worse than the loss of the ball, so the other boys quickly agreed to allow Andrew to play. Although their father expected them home, Sylvia stood on the other side of the fence watching the game, her heart swelling with pride.

As autumn waned, Sylvia watched as Richard and Andrew became fast friends. Andrew was as skinny and filthy as ever, but he smiled more, and although he was still quiet around the other children, sometimes he would whisper a joke that would leave Richard howling with laughter. When she spotted Andrew on the schoolyard wearing a jacket Richard had outgrown, she did not need to ask how he had come by it. At home Richard spoke about his friend so often that their father encouraged him to invite Andrew over to play. One day Andrew was waiting with Richard at the gate when his sisters came to escort him home.

"Andrew's coming over to play," Richard informed them. "And he's staying for dinner."

"Oh, really?" said Claudia. "Does Father know?"

"It'll be fine," Sylvia interjected. She smiled at the wary little boy. "Father has asked Richard to invite him many times."

"Do his parents know?" Claudia asked dubiously.

"They won't mind," Andrew piped up. Sylvia was sure they would not. She doubted anyone would even notice whether he returned home.

After that, Andrew came home with Richard nearly every day. Sometimes Sylvia gently probed him with questions about his home and his family, but Andrew said little. Still, his guarded replies were enough for Sylvia to deduce that he was unhappy and worried about his little sister. Sylvia did not know what to do. Extracting details from Andrew was so difficult that she was unsure just how bad things were, and she did not want to do anything to compel him to run away, as so many other children had when their fathers lost their jobs and their mothers could not feed them. An unhappy home was safer than the life on the rails so many other men and boys had chosen. So Sylvia found reasons to give Andrew the sturdy clothes Richard had outgrown but not worn out, and she filled her brother's lunch box each morning with food enough for two boys. Andrew began to fill out, and he must have begun brushing his hair and washing his hands and face at school. Sylvia suspected that a kindhearted teacher had taken an interest in his welfare, but Claudia teased that the young boy had taken it upon himself to improve his appearance because he had a crush on Sylvia.

When winter snows began to fall, Sylvia's thoughts turned to Christmas. That winter would bring their fifth Christmas without Mama. Every year since she had left them, the Bergstroms had celebrated in a subdued fashion, in part because of their reduced circumstances, but also because Sylvia's father was the head of the household and his heart simply wasn't in it. He found no joy in the old Bergstrom traditions without his beloved wife by his side, and his daughters found it difficult to keep them on their own. When Sylvia thought of Andrew, though, she decided that even a quiet Bergstrom holiday would likely surpass any warmth and happiness he might find at home. They must invite him to spend Christmas Eve and Christmas Day with their family because if anyone needed the joy and hope of the season, Andrew did.

It was Claudia, however, who came to Sylvia with the notion that they must bring back the old Bergstrom traditions in all their splendor. Sylvia was dubious. How could they afford to rival lavish Christmases past? How could they proceed without their mother's guiding hand? She hesitated to voice aloud her sense that it was wrong, somehow, to enjoy the holiday without their mother.

As the days passed, Claudia wore her down with her persistence, and finally reminded her that if they did not restore their traditions, no one would, and all the Bergstrom stories would be lost. Richard's memories of their mother had grown dim. He had been so young when she died, and their brokenhearted father could rarely bring himself to speak of her. The sisters owed it to Richard and their mother to fill in the spaces of their younger brother's memory with their own.

Sylvia, who would do anything for her darling little brother, needed no further inducement to join Claudia in reviving their family's traditions. Their father was surprisingly willing to go along with the plan. "It's been too long since we've had a truly Merry Christmas around here," he said, smiling wistfully at his daughters. He opened his billfold and paid them a special "Christmas allowance" to spend on their celebration — modest, but still more than they had hoped for. The sisters decided to spend it upon gifts for their father, Richard, Andrew, Andrew's little sister, and ingredients for their favorite Christmas treats — Great-Aunt Lucinda's German cookies and the famous Bergstrom strudel. As they made their preparations, the holiday spirit returned to the home, so gradually and quietly that it came as an unexpected delight when Sylvia discovered Lucinda whistling a Christmas carol as she folded the laundry, or caught Uncle William and Aunt Nellie kissing beneath a sprig of mistletoe. Great-Aunt Lydia took them shopping for gifts and groceries, and in the week before Christmas, Elm Creek Manor was once again filled with the aromas of gingerbread, anise, and cinnamon. Sylvia and Claudia wrapped store-bought presents for the boys and their father, and made gifts for the rest of the family.

It felt like Christmas again. Until the joy and hope of the season had been restored to her, Sylvia had not realized how much her heart had longed for them.

If only Mama were there.

★ ★ ★

On the day before Christmas Eve, Sylvia and Richard were upstairs in the nursery playing baseball with a broom handle and a bundle of knotted socks when Claudia entered. "I need you in the kitchen," she told her sister. "It's time to start the strudel."

"I'll be down in a minute." Sylvia caught a grounder and tagged out Richard before he reached first. "The inning's almost over."

Richard trotted back to home plate and picked up the fallen broom handle. "No, it's not. I still have two more outs."

Sylvia grinned and wound up to pitch. "Like I said, I'll be down in a minute."

"We need to start now, while the kitchen's free." Claudia's nose wrinkled in disapproval as she observed the game. "You shouldn't play baseball in the house anyway."

"It's not a real baseball." Sylvia tossed the knot of socks toward her brother, who swung the broom handle, connected, and sent the makeshift ball careening toward left field.

"It's a sockball," said Richard helpfully as he ran for first base.

"Whatever it is, it could still break something." Claudia turned for the door. "If you can't be bothered to help, I'll do it myself."

Sylvia could imagine the disaster that would ensue if she allowed that to happen. "No, wait. I'm coming." She scooped up the sockball and lofted it to Richard, who caught it easily. "Sorry. I'll have to finish you off later."

"Says you." Richard grinned and went off to play with his model airplanes.

"We couldn't have waited ten minutes?" Sylvia asked as she followed her sister downstairs.

"Great-Aunt Lucinda just finished her last batch of cookies but she'll need us out of the way when it's time to make supper. She said we may make strudel now or not at all."

Sylvia knew that was a valid reason for haste, but couldn't admit it. "You could have said so before."

"You didn't give me a chance. You were too busy arguing for your right to play 'sockball.' "

Sylvia clamped her mouth around a retort. She wouldn't be the one to start a fight, not so close to Christmas, not with the family seeming more content than they had been in years.

She hoped allowing Claudia the last word would put her in a sweeter temper, but in the kitchen, Claudia became even more imperious. She sent Sylvia down into the cellar to fetch a basket of apples, a task they had always handled together. When Sylvia returned, huffing from exertion, she found Claudia taking flour, sugar, nuts, and spices from the pantry — and wearing their mother's best apron.

"What's that you're wearing?" she demanded, setting down the basket with a thud.

Claudia glanced down at her clothes. "It's an apron, of course. You should put yours on, too, or your dress will get covered in flour."

"That's Mama's apron."

Claudia regarded Sylvia with exasperation. "You know my old one is worn out. Aunt Lucinda said I should wear this one. If it bothers you so much, you can wear it and I'll wear yours."

"Never mind," muttered Sylvia, taking two paring knives from the drawer.

Claudia sighed and shook her head. "When you're done being ridiculous, would you please bring a sheet from the linen closet?"

"Why don't you do it?"

"Because I'm doing this." Claudia indicated the pastry ingredients in her arms. "Why are you being so disagreeable?"

"Why are you being so bossy?"

It was a charge Claudia hated, perhaps because she knew how often her behavior merited it. "I'm not being bossy. I just want to make sure this is done right. Don't you see? It's up to us to make this a happy Christmas for everyone. If we can't do it this year, they might not give us another chance."

"They can't cancel Christmas."

Claudia nudged the basket of apples closer to the kitchen table with her foot and set her burdens on the counter. "No, but they can tell us not to try, and then we can go back to the same gloomy Christmases we've had for the past four years. Is that what you want? More importantly, do you think that's what Mama would want?"

Claudia began flinging handfuls of flour into a mixing bowl, her mouth in a defiant line. Sylvia watched her for a moment, then, without another word of complaint, she hurried upstairs, retrieved a clean sheet from the linen closet, and draped it over the long wooden table as their mother had always done, and other women of the family had done before her. She pulled the thin fabric smooth and fastened the corners to the legs of the table with clothespins. As she dusted the sheet with flour, Claudia cautioned, "Not so much." Sylvia said not a word in reply.

They took turns kneading the dough — pressing it into the floured board with the heels of their hands, folding it over, turning it, pressing again. Sylvia was surprised how quickly her arms tired from the effort. It had not seemed so difficult in years past — but she and her sister had never kneaded the dough for more than a minute or two at a time, as one of the elder Bergstrom women had always shouldered the burden of the chore. After ten minutes had elapsed, Sylvia suggested they set the dough aside to rest, but Claudia insisted they continue for another two minutes apiece. Sylvia was tempted to tell her to do all four of the minutes herself if she felt that strongly about them, but she bit her tongue and did her share.

Finally Claudia divided the smooth ball of dough into two halves, separated them on the floured board, and covered them with a flick of the dishtowel that reminded Sylvia, painfully, of a similar gesture their mother used to make. How pleased she would be to see her two daughters working together to make the famous Bergstrom strudel, Sylvia thought, and she resolved to finish the task in a manner that would make their mother proud.

Yet no matter how agreeably Sylvia followed the directions her sister unnecessarily provided, the more Claudia chided her. Sylvia took off too much apple flesh with the peel. She was not peeling fast enough, and the apples would turn brown before they could be baked. She sliced the apples too thin. She did not chop the nuts finely enough. With every word of criticism, Sylvia's temper flared, but she would not allow Claudia to provoke her into an outburst, ruining what should have been a significant moment in the history of their family. The two Bergstrom sisters were renewing a beloved tradition they had last shared with their mother, a tradition that reached back into the past to the first Bergstroms to come to America and possibly even earlier.

On behalf of all the Bergstrom women who had preceded them, it was essential that they work together. Especially when the apples were prepared and it was time to stretch the dough. Especially since they would be spending many hours together to make the ten strudel Claudia had decided they needed that Christmas, one for the family and nine to give away.

"It's rested enough," remarked Claudia as she pulled back the dishtowel covering the two flattened balls of dough. Sylvia, who had observed the making of strudel nearly as many times as her elder sister and knew as well as she did how long the dough needed to rest, merely murmured her assent. She was reminded of how graciously their mother had always asked the opinion of the other women and girls present, even her novice daughters, achieving consensus before deciding it was time to stretch the dough.

Claudia rolled out the ball of dough into a rectangle, then beckoned Sylvia forward to help stretch. Sylvia obliged, and in unison, they reached beneath the dough and pulled it toward themselves with the back of their hands. When Claudia stepped to her right, Sylvia mirrored her, so they always faced each other on opposite sides of the table. At first, Sylvia was amazed by how quickly the familiar motions came back to her, and as the sisters fell into a rhythm of reaching and stretching, she once again marveled at the dough's transformation from a smooth ball into a thin, translucent sheet.

She was so involved in the methodical process that it was Claudia who first noticed the trouble. "This isn't right," she muttered.

"What? There aren't any tears."

"No, but we haven't made it any wider or thinner for quite a while."

Sylvia had paid little attention to the time. She could not honestly say how much progress they had made in the last two minutes, or the last five. "It seems fine to me."

"The dough should have reached the edges of the table by now." Claudia paused, wiped a smear of flour from her face with the back of her hand, and studied the dough. "Something's wrong."

"Did you count how many handfuls of flour you used?"

"Yes."

"Did you use the usual cup for measuring the water?"

"Yes, of course," snapped Claudia impatiently. "I did all that."

"We could give it another few minutes," suggested Sylvia. "Or we could ask Aunt Lucinda —"

"No. We need to do this on our own, remember?" Claudia slid her hands beneath the dough and indicated with a sharp nod that Sylvia was to do the same. Sylvia complied, and this time when she released the dough and allowed it to fall back to the table, she noticed that instead of draping gracefully across the floured sheet, it sprang back slightly, like a rubber band.

Claudia was watching her face. “That time you saw it, too.”

Sylvia nodded as they reached beneath the dough again. Lift, stretch, fall — and again, that almost imperceptible motion of the dough as it sprang back into its former shape. Their mother’s dough had never done that. Neither had their grandmother’s. “It’s . . . rubbery,” said Sylvia, searching for the least offensive term.

“I made it exactly the same as always,” said Claudia. “You saw me.”

That Sylvia had been out of the kitchen for most of the time Claudia mixed the dough was hardly worth mentioning given the mounting problems at hand. Sylvia could now see that while the dough was suitably thin in the center, the outer edge of the rectangle was as thick as a fist, as if it were a heavy frame around a delicate canvas.

“I think somehow we have to stretch the edges more without stretching the center,” Sylvia finally said.

"And how are we supposed to do that?"

"I don't know *how;* I just know *what.*"

"That's not very helpful," grumbled Claudia, but after a moment, she took up the rolling pin and tried to flatten the edges. It helped somewhat, and after Claudia had made two trips around the perimeter with the rolling pin, she told Sylvia to resume stretching. "Harder this time."

"Are you sure?" asked Sylvia. "The center is already so thin."

"Yes, I'm sure." To demonstrate, Claudia thrust her hands beneath the dough and pulled firmly toward the edges — and gasped in horror as a long tear running the length of the rectangle appeared on Sylvia's side of the table.

"We can patch it," said Sylvia, already setting to it.

"If you had pulled equally from your side —"

"You didn't give me a chance! The tear still would have happened, just in a different place."

"Never mind." Claudia came around the table to the other end of the tear and began pinching it closed. "Let's just fix it. There's no need to place blame."

Apparently there wasn't, Sylvia thought,

unless she was at fault. But she said nothing as the sisters worked from the ends toward the middle until the tear was mended with a seam of pinched dough. Afterward, Claudia circled the rectangle one last time, trimming off the thick frame with a knife.

"What are you doing?" asked Sylvia. On every side, the dough rectangle fell several inches short of the edge of the table.

"It wasn't going to stretch any farther."

"It's not big enough."

"But it is almost thin enough, and it will taste the same."

Sylvia wasn't so sure. What if whatever alchemy had made the dough more difficult to stretch had also affected its flavor? "I'll get the apples," she said instead, careful to allow no trace of annoyance or worry into her voice. At least they would have extra noodles for soup.

The dough rolled around the apples as easily as ever, to their unspoken relief, and soon their first strudel was baking in the oven. They did not have nearly as much difficulty stretching the second ball of dough — in part because they had learned from their mistakes and took care not to leave a thick rope of dough around a thin center rectangle — but when they could stretch the dough no more, it still was thicker than their mother's, and it did not come within two inches of the table's edges.

Still, the first strudel came out of the oven a beautiful golden brown, and the aroma of baked apples and cinnamon drew other members of the family into the kitchen. Most of them praised the sisters and declared that they couldn't wait to taste the strudel on Christmas morning, but Uncle William took one look at their first attempt cooling on the table and said, "Looks like the runt of the litter."

"We won't bother saving any for you, then," Sylvia teased right back, but Claudia busied herself at the sink full of dishes until he left the kitchen so he would not see her scarlet face.

"Eight more to go," Sylvia remarked on her way to the cellar for more apples.

"Maybe two are enough," said Claudia wearily.

Sylvia stopped short on the stairs. "You don't mean that. Uncle William was just teasing."

"No, it's not that. I suppose I had no idea how difficult this would be without —" Claudia composed herself. "Even when Mama was ill, she managed everything with such ease. Next year — maybe next year we can try to do more."

Sylvia was surprised by her sister's admission of weakness, or at least the closest thing to an admission of weakness Claudia was likely to let slip. As for herself, she hated to abandon any task until she had no choice but to admit defeat — but she also did not relish the thought of spending the rest of the day in the kitchen. The temptation to leave the kitchen overruled her perseverance, and so Sylvia agreed that the two strudel they had already made would be sufficient, as it meant one for the Bergstroms and one for Andrew to take home to his family. Their friends and neighbors had not received the famous Bergstrom strudel since Eleanor's last Christmas and would not expect it this season. Next year, Sylvia and Claudia promised each other, they would be pleasantly surprised.

The next morning, Christmas Eve morning, Andrew arrived at the back door while the Bergstroms were finishing breakfast. Sylvia's father, who had planned to pick him up later that afternoon in the car, joked that the boy's haste would do nothing to speed Santa's visit, but as the boy cast a longing gaze toward the remains of the meal, there could be no mistaking what had sped him to their door. Lucinda welcomed him to the table and signaled for Claudia to bring an extra plate, and soon the scrawny boy was bolting down everything they set before him.

After breakfast the boys ran off to play. The women tidied the kitchen then sent Uncle William and Aunt Nellie out to find a tree. "Isn't anyone else in this family ever going to get married?" Uncle William grumbled as he shrugged into his coat.

"Don't look at me," said Lucinda.

He peered hopefully at Claudia. "How old are you again?"

"Sixteen," she said, straightening proudly.

"Forget it, Will," said her father. "The job is yours for at least ten more years."

"Daddy," protested Claudia.

"We don't mind," Aunt Nellie assured the girls' father. She linked her arm through her husband's and smiled up at him. "In fact, this year, we're going to pick out the best tree Elm Creek Manor has ever had."

The couple left through the back door, following a trail broken through the soft layer of snow on their way toward the bridge over Elm Creek. Watching through the kitchen window, Lucinda remarked to

Sylvia's father, "Looks like it's going to be another four-hour search this year."

"I'm sure William hopes so," he replied, grinning.

"Well, the ornaments are ready in the ballroom," said Claudia, missing the implications. "Whenever they do get back, we can begin decorating."

"In the meantime, I'll fix lunch," said Lucinda.

Claudia nodded. "And I have some sewing to do."

Sylvia had small gifts to wrap, knitted socks and scarves she had completed the night before. She left her festive packages in the ballroom, not surprised to find that her aunt and uncle had not returned, then went looking for Claudia. Her sister sat in the front parlor, in their mother's favorite chair, threading a needle. At her feet lay piles of fabric she had sorted by color.

"What are you working on?" Sylvia drew closer to the familiar-looking scraps. "Is that the Christmas Quilt?"

Claudia nodded, holding the needle between pursed lips while she tied a knot at the end of the thread.

Sylvia looked from the triangles on her sister's lap to the stack of Feathered Star blocks on the table at her right hand.

"Those pieces are too big for a Feathered Star. They should be less than half that size."

"I'm not making Feathered Stars." Claudia took the needle from her mouth and speared its tip into a white triangle and a green one. She nodded to their mother's old sewing basket, which she had long ago adopted. Upon its open lid Sylvia spied a few red-and-green Variable Star blocks.

Sylvia picked up one and immediately spotted the mistakes. The tip of one star point had been lopped off by an adjoining seam. A pair of green star points did not meet at the tip of the central red square. On the back of the block, instead of pressing her seams flat and smooth, Claudia had folded them over carelessly, creating a thick lump of fabric layers that would be difficult to quilt through later. Sylvia compared the block to a second.

"Did you do this on purpose?" asked Sylvia, matching the top corners of the blocks and holding them together to estimate the difference in size. "Did you mean for this one to be a half-inch smaller than the other?"

Claudia snatched the blocks from her grasp. "Don't be ridiculous. I used the same templates for all of them."

She must have varied her seam allowances, then. "You'll have to block them with the iron. You'll need a lot of steam —"

"I know how to block a quilt."

"You could have avoided that step if you had sewed more accurately. Why are you making Variable Stars instead of —" Sylvia broke off, remembering just in time that the last thing she wanted to do was encourage her sister to attempt a far more difficult pattern when she could barely manage one of the simplest star blocks in her repertoire. "If you try to sew these blocks together, you'll be able to match up either the star points or the corners, but not both. Does Aunt Lucinda know what you're up to? She won't appreciate it if you ruin her quilt."

"I will not ruin her quilt, and yes, I already asked her if I might finish it."

"And she said yes?"

"Of course she said yes, or I wouldn't be sitting here working on it. Honestly, Sylvia."

Sylvia thought of the time and talent their mother and Great-Aunt Lucinda had sewn into their Feathered Stars and holly plumes. All of their work would go to waste if Claudia distorted their handiwork with her poorly constructed Variable Stars. "Maybe you should let me help."

"Maybe you should find something of your own to work on."

Why should she? The Christmas Quilt was as much hers as it was Claudia's. "If I make some of the blocks, we'll finish more quickly. That way you'll also have an example to follow when you're steaming or trimming your blocks to the right size. I think your trouble is your seam allowances —"

"My trouble is that I have an annoying little sister who doesn't have anything better to do on Christmas Eve than criticize me. Great-Aunt Lucinda said I could finish the quilt and that's what I'm going to do. You're just angry because you didn't think of it first. If you had, you wouldn't have let me help you, and you know it."

Every word struck home, and Sylvia's temper flared. In the distance she heard the double doors to the foyer slam, followed by the happy clamor of voices. Uncle William and Aunt Nellie had returned with a tree and the sisters were needed in the ballroom, but Sylvia couldn't resist one parting shot: "The word 'variable' in your 'Variable Stars' shouldn't refer to their size."

She hurried from the parlor before Claudia could have the last word.

Richard and Andrew must have flown down from the nursery. She tried to keep them out of the way as Uncle William and her father hauled the tree into the ballroom and set it up in its familiar place on the dais. Great-Aunt Lucinda brought in trays of food so they could lunch while they trimmed the tree, and someone switched on the radio. Suddenly the room was filled with music and laughter, and Sylvia felt a pang of longing for her mother. Her eyes met her father's, and she knew he shared her thoughts. In his arms he carried the paper angels she and Claudia had made years before in Sunday school. He put Claudia's on a high branch and placed Sylvia's exactly even on the opposite side of the tree — not one branch higher, not one lower. His great deliberation signaled to Sylvia that he had seen Claudia's stormy expression and had identified Sylvia as its source.

She flushed guiltily and looked away, pretending to be absorbed in the boys' antics as they wrapped garlands of popcorn and cranberries around the lower branches of the tree. *Wait until she finishes piecing the top of the Christmas Quilt and wants help layering and basting it,* Sylvia thought bitterly. Sylvia would not lift a finger or a needle to help her. And she was through with letting Claudia carry on as if she were the lady of the house. If anyone held that role with Mama gone, it was Great-Aunt Lucinda, not a silly sixteen-year-old girl.

The tree was all but finished when Great-Aunt Lucinda noted that someone ought to hide the star. "I'll do it," said Claudia, smiling as she removed the eight-pointed ruby-and-gold star from its box.

"No, I will," said Sylvia, snatching it from her hand.

"You could do it together," their father and Lucinda said in unison.

Sylvia smothered a groan. "I'll be right back," she said, and she raced from the room before Claudia or anyone else could object.

But where to hide the star? She would have been tempted to choose an especially difficult hiding place for the pleasure of tormenting her sister, but she suddenly doubted Claudia would take up the search. Richard was younger, but that did not mean Sylvia should choose a more obvious location for his sake. He knew all the manor's secret places and would be disappointed if he found the star too soon. Then

Sylvia remembered Andrew, and she decided that she wanted him to win. Even the competitive Richard would be pleased if his friend won the game and could add a prize to the gifts Santa would leave for him beneath the Bergstroms' tree.

Perhaps Sylvia could help him in the search the way cousin Elizabeth had once helped her. Andrew had no pillow of his own in the Bergstroms' home to look beneath, and he was not likely to run crying to Richard's room as Sylvia had fled to hers so many years before. Andrew spent most of his time at Elm Creek Manor in the nursery. Perhaps, if that was where he felt most comfortable, he would begin his search there.

Taking the steps two at a time, Sylvia raced upstairs to the third floor and burst into the nursery. Andrew loved Richard's model trains. Sylvia hurried across the room and hid the star in the wooden crate that held the engine and its cars, leaving only one golden tip visible.

She returned to the ballroom, pleased with herself, but her satisfaction fled with one look from her father. She glanced at Great-Aunt Lucinda, who shook her head even though a faint smile quirked at her lips.

"I hid the star," she announced, managing a weak grin. Her father sent the younger children out to search for it, and Sylvia busied herself with rearranging a few of the ornaments upon the tree, more to conceal her blush than any aesthetic purpose. She resolved to avoid provoking Claudia or anyone else until Christmas was over. With any luck, the sight of her snatching the star from her sister's hand would fade from the adults' memories. She knew Claudia would never forget.

They finished trimming the tree, all but the very highest bough, and then they were left with nothing to do but listen to the radio, admire the tree, and chat, as no triumphant child had returned with the glass star held tightly in a small fist. "You did hide it *in* the manor, right, Sylvia?" asked Uncle William after an hour had passed. "You didn't throw it out a window into a snowbank?"

"It's in the manor," said Sylvia, glancing toward the door worriedly. At first she had hoped only Andrew would find the star; now she would be glad if anyone did.

"Did you hide it where a child would think to look?" asked Claudia. Her tone, her stance, her look of disappointed resignation pointedly telegraphed that she was not at all surprised her younger sister had found a way to ruin a beloved holiday tradition. If Claudia had been allowed to hide the star, it would be shining on the top of the tree by now.

"Of course." The crate of model trains was right there on the floor of the nursery, not on a high shelf or tucked away in a closet. Surely she had not hidden it too well.

Just then the ballroom door burst open. "We can't find it," said Richard, panting from his sprint through the manor.

"It's a big house," said Uncle William. "Keep looking."

Richard shrugged and ran off again. "Maybe I should give them a hint," Sylvia appealed to her father. At his assent, she dashed after Richard and told him to look on the third floor — and to make sure he passed the message along to the other children. He promised, grinning because his sister knew him so well, and soon the ballroom echoed with the thunder of many feet racing up the stairs.

A half hour later, Richard returned to the ballroom, Andrew at his heels. "When you said third floor, did you mean the attic? Because I thought we weren't allowed up there."

Claudia whirled on her sister. "You didn't put it in the attic, did you? Someone could get hurt on those stairs."

"No! Richard, the attic would be the fourth floor. Did you try the nursery?"

"Yes. Everyone's been in the nursery for at least an hour."

Sylvia knew he was exaggerating, since it had been only a half hour ago that she had given him the hint. Even so, with so many children in the nursery, someone should have stumbled upon the star within minutes.

With Richard and Andrew leading the way, Sylvia, Claudia, their father, and Great-Aunt Lucinda climbed the stairs to the third floor. The nursery lay directly above the library — an unfortunate oversight in planning that Sylvia's grandfather had not noticed until the first time his reading was disturbed by noisy play overhead. Like the library, the nursery stretched the entire width of the south wing and welcomed in sunlight through east, west, and south facing windows. In the twilight, large flakes of snow blew against the glass, but the children were too busy playing to notice. Uncle William's daughter served tea to Sylvia's old dolls, two boys were engaged in a battle with

Richard's toy soldiers, and other cousins read or built block towers or played games of their own invention. After an hour and a half of fruitless searching, perseverance had finally succumbed to the allure of toys. The quest for the star had been abandoned.

But no child was playing with the model trains.

"You haven't given up already, have you?" asked Sylvia. The little girl cousin to whom she had given the Nine-Patch quilt looked up and smiled, but the other children were too engrossed in their play to hear.

"Perhaps another hint is in order," suggested Lucinda. "Animal, vegetable, or mineral?"

Richard and Andrew looked up at Sylvia, hopeful.

"Mineral," she said. "A form of transportation." The two boys began to wander the room, moving aside scattered toys, heading in the opposite direction from the crate of model trains. "Think of something used to transport passengers or cargo over long distances. Oh, for heaven's sake." Desperate to salvage the game, she made train noises, mimed the movement of wheels, and tugged on the cord of an imaginary steam whistle.

Richard brightened and ran across the room to his model trains, Andrew right behind. They dug through the crate, emptying it of engines and boxcars with amazing speed, until the last one lay on the floor. The boys looked across the room at Sylvia, expectant and puzzled.

"Great hint," Claudia scoffed. "You sent them to the wrong place."

But she hadn't. Quickly Sylvia joined the boys and peered into the crate to see for herself. It was empty.

Lucinda saw trouble in her expression. "This is where you hid the star?"

Sylvia nodded, puzzled. She scanned the clutter of train cars to see if the star had accidentally been set aside in the boys' haste, but it was not there. "I don't understand. I put it right here."

"Among the trains," said Claudia, skeptical. "Then where is it?"

"I don't know."

"Are you sure you hid it here?" asked her father. "Perhaps you had second thoughts and returned later to move it to a more difficult hiding place. Think hard."

"I'm certain." The question stung. She wouldn't have forgotten where she had hidden the star.

"Perhaps someone else moved it." Aunt Lucinda raised her eyebrows at Richard. "As a little Christmas joke?"

Richard's eyes went wide and innocent. "Not me."

Andrew shook his head vigorously, his expression terrified.

Sylvia knew that, like her, her father and Great-Aunt Lucinda had instantly conjured up images of what punishments a prankster might face in Andrew's house. She forced a smile. "It's a very funny joke," she said, and made herself laugh. Her father let out a chuckle, and the fear in Andrew's eyes relaxed.

"I don't think it's funny at all," declared Claudia.

"Okay, young man." Great-Aunt Lucinda smiled and held out her palm to Richard. "You had us fooled, but now the joke's over."

Richard frowned. "I told you I didn't touch it." Suddenly he looked excited. "Hey, what if a ghost did it? A spirit like in that Christmas story Sylvia read me last night."

Andrew's frightened expression returned. "He's just teasing," Sylvia hastened to reassure him. She believed that Richard had not taken the star, but then, who had? She searched the other children's faces for a clue, but they played on, barely paying attention to the drama unfolding by the model trains. Not a trace of guilt or glee colored their expressions.

"Richard, why don't you put away your trains now," advised Sylvia's father. As Andrew joined in to help, Sylvia's father beckoned the women out of their hearing. "Perhaps the star was found — and broken before the finder could return to the ballroom. It's surprising it hasn't happened sooner."

"I always did think it was a bad idea to send children running through the house with a glass star," mused Lucinda. "It's possible, perhaps even likely. But the question remains, who?"

"Not Richard," said Sylvia, eager to exonerate her brother. She knew instinctively that he had spoken the truth. "Could it be Andrew?"

"What makes you think so?" asked her father.

"Because he was the most likely to find the star," Sylvia explained, reluctant to direct blame toward a boy who, as far as she knew, had never broken a single rule in his many visits to the Bergstrom home. "I hid the star among the trains because the nursery is his favorite place in the manor and the trains are his favorite toys. I wanted to help him find the star as cousin Elizabeth helped me."

"You mean as cousin Elizabeth helped you *cheat,*" said Claudia. "Anyway, the nursery isn't Andrew's favorite place in the manor. The kitchen is."

Sylvia wished she had considered that because, of course, Claudia was right.

Great-Aunt Lucinda shook her head. "If the star was broken, I doubt Andrew did it. Remember when he broke that glass on the veranda after I warned the boys not to put them down in the line of fire of their marbles? He picked up every shard, brought them to me, and apologized. He would have done the same thing here."

"This isn't a drinking glass, one of many," said Claudia. "This is a family heirloom."

Sylvia's father nodded, thoughtful, and called the children over. When they had gathered around him, he tried to tease the truth out of them, but no one admitted to finding the star. In a voice too low for anyone but Sylvia and Lucinda to hear, Claudia muttered that he ought to threaten them with a spanking, but Sylvia thought his disarming humor was the right approach. Even Andrew was smiling. But even Sylvia had to admit that her father's questions yielded little useful information. The timeline of the children's whereabouts that he managed to piece together told them nothing more than that all of the children had been in most of the rooms of the manor at some point during the search, sometimes alone, but most often in the company of at least one other child.

Eventually Sylvia's father must have decided that the perpetrator needed a stronger motivation to confess. "If no one has found the star," he warned, "no one can collect the prize."

"There's a prize?" said Andrew.

Richard nodded. "It's usually a toy or candy."

Andrew nudged him. "Come on. Let's keep looking."

Sylvia's heart went out to him. He of all the children wanted a prize so badly that he would continue searching despite the obvious futility of the task. As badly as the game had turned out, she did not regret her attempt to help him. "Can't we let them share the prize?" she asked her father.

"That's against the rules," said Claudia.

Their father held up his hands, somber.

"Claudia's right. We won't be able to put the star on top of the tree tonight, so we can't award the prize. I'm disappointed no one wants to come forward and tell the truth, and I'm sure Santa Claus isn't very happy, either."

The children exchanged looks of surprise and dismay, but no one looked any more guilty or worried than the others.

"I'll tell you what we can do," her father continued. "If the star is on the kitchen table tomorrow morning in time for breakfast, I won't ask who left it there, and everyone can share the prize equally."

"Is it candy?" piped up one of the youngest cousins.

"It is," said Sylvia's father. "Now, let's go downstairs and enjoy the rest of our Christmas Eve. It's almost bedtime."

When they returned to the ballroom without the star for the top of the tree, Sylvia's father treated the astonished adults to a lighthearted account of the missing star and repeated his promise to the children. Then he read aloud "A Visit from St. Nicholas" as he had done every Christmas for as long as Sylvia could remember. Afterward, he gave up his chair to Aunt Nellie, who read St. Luke's account of the Nativity.

When she finished, the children rose from their places around the tree to collect hugs and kisses before going off to bed. Gazing at their sweet, beloved faces, Sylvia could not believe any of them capable of hiding a guilty secret. "I wish Father would have let them have the prize anyway," she said with a sigh.

She had only been thinking aloud, but Claudia heard her. "If you wanted them to have the prize so badly, you should have let them find the star."

"I tried. I hid it, and obviously someone found it."

"So you say."

Sylvia stared at her. "Do you think I still have it?"

"I think you know where it is."

"I don't," Sylvia retorted. "I haven't the faintest idea where it could be. One of the children probably broke it and is too upset to confess, just as Father said."

Claudia searched her face, frowning. "If that's so, then where are the pieces? I intend to search every dustbin and look beneath every carpet. None of the children has left the manor since before the search began. If the star is broken, the pieces must be here. And if they aren't —"

Claudia left the words unspoken as she

volunteered to help the aunts put the children to bed. At first Sylvia was too stunned to follow, but then she steeled herself with a deep breath and offered to see to Richard and Andrew. After she had supervised their teeth-brushing, heard their prayers, and tucked them into the twin beds in Richard's room, she crept upstairs to the nursery. She discovered Claudia rummaging through the dustbin.

"Any luck?" asked Sylvia quietly.

Claudia shook her head.

Together they searched every place a frantic child might have hidden the ruby-and-gold shards of broken glass. Claudia seemed glad to have her sister there — not because she wanted the company, but to assure herself that Sylvia could not dispose of the star, whole or in pieces, while unobserved. It was late when they gave up, and Claudia was even angrier than when they had begun. Sylvia began to wish that she *had* kept the star. She would have confessed to it then and there just to make peace with her sister on Christmas Eve.

"We should go to bed," she said tiredly. "Everyone else has, and it's possible whoever took it is waiting until everyone is asleep to leave it on the kitchen table."

Claudia folded her arms. "So that's how

you're going to end this charade."

Sylvia was too exhausted to argue. "Oh, stop it, Claudia."

She left her sister standing there and went off to bed.

Christmas morning dawned silvery white. Sylvia woke to the sound of hushed voices and quick footsteps passing in the hall outside her door. Smiling, she rose and dressed for church in a green velvet dress Claudia had outgrown. It had been Claudia's best dress, worn only on special occasions, and Great-Aunt Lucinda had helped Sylvia make it over so that it fit her properly and looked almost like new. She brushed her hair and tied it back with a matching ribbon. Sometimes, if she looked in the mirror at precisely the right angle, she thought she looked almost as pretty as her sister. Standing far away from the mirror helped.

She greeted Aunt Nellie in passing as she hurried downstairs, eager to reach the kitchen, certain that the Christmas star would be on the table. From the foot of the stairs, she spied a cluster of cousins still clad in their pajamas gathered around the door to the ballroom. Every Christmas Eve, Great-Aunt Lucinda locked the door before retiring for the night so no one would disturb Santa if he came by, but the children always checked in case she had forgotten. Richard had his eye to the keyhole. "I can't see anything," Sylvia heard him say. "The lights are out. Quit shoving! Wait a minute — I think — yes! There's something under the tree!"

The other children pressed closer. "What?" Andrew cried. "What do you see?"

"Just shadows. It's too dark to see anything more. Keep your voices down. We're not supposed to peek."

"That's right," said Sylvia. The children jumped guiltily and stepped away from the door, all save Richard, who barely glanced up from the keyhole. "You should be getting dressed for church. I bet that's where your parents think you are."

"Can't we open the door and look to make sure Santa came?" asked one of the younger cousins. "We won't step even one little baby toe into the room."

The other children joined in, begging for just one look, just to be sure. Sylvia held up her hands, laughing, glad that it wasn't her decision. She would be tempted to let the children tear into their gifts right away, even if it made them late for church. "Do you really all have such guilty consciences?" she teased. "You really aren't sure whether Santa put you on his 'Good' list?"

She scooted them toward the stairs and waited at the bottom until the last reluctant straggler had reached the landing. Then, with one last entreaty to hurry, she continued toward the kitchen.

She met her father in the hallway. His expression told her what she needed to know, but still she asked, "Was it there?"

Her father shook his head. "They still have time. I said in time for breakfast, and we won't have breakfast until after church."

Sylvia nodded, but she could sense that his concern ran deep. Bergstrom children were raised to respect their elders and to do as they were told. Such blatant defiance of her father's wishes was unthinkable. Like children everywhere, the Bergstroms broke rules and made mistakes — Sylvia was proof enough of that — but they never failed to accept the consequences of their actions, even if, deep down, they wouldn't admit that they had done anything wrong. The taking of the star and the refusal to return it, even broken, was something new and disturbing in their household.

The adults stayed away from the kitchen

as they helped the children dress in their finest for church services, offering the guilty child every opportunity to return the star unobserved. The children were so excited they could hardly stand still long enough to have their hair combed, and more than once, Sylvia had caught an older cousin sneaking off to test the doorknob to the ballroom.

As members of the choir, Sylvia and Claudia were expected to arrive at church a half hour before services to don their robes and warm up their voices. Richard and Andrew rode with Sylvia in the backseat when Father drove her and Claudia to the same church in Waterford their family had attended for generations. By the time the sisters filed out of the music room and climbed the stairs to the loft with the rest of the choir, the pews were nearly full. Sylvia spotted the rest of the family among the throng, but she was disappointed not to find Andrew's parents and little sister.

She soon forgot their absence in the glory of the day. Her heart filled with joy and gratitude as she sang the traditional carols she loved so dearly. How the Lord must have loved the people of the world to send them His only Son! And how He must love them still, despite their sin, despite their weakness, despite the shadow of the Cross that fell upon the Manger even on this most joyous of days. At that moment Sylvia felt touched by the light of grace, and she knew that if she could remember that feeling after she left that gathering, even in her darkest hours, she would never be alone.

The feeling of joyful gratitude lasted throughout the service and soared when the entire congregation rose after the final blessing and sang "Joy to the World" as the church bells pealed an accompaniment. The service ended, but still the congregants lingered, wishing one another a Merry Christmas. Every embrace, every greeting was a prayer for good health and peace in the coming year. Sylvia spotted Claudia putting away her choir robe with the other sopranos. She scrambled down the risers and flung her arms around her sister.

"Merry Christmas, Claudia," she said, her voice muffled by her billowing robe.

"What's the matter with you?" Claudia exclaimed. "You scared me half to death." Beside her, her friends smirked. They had known Claudia too long to be surprised by the antics of her difficult little sister.

Sylvia ignored them. "I just want you to know that I love you."

"Well, I love you, too, of course, but I don't have to tackle you in the choir loft to prove it."

"Maybe you should just send her a Christmas card next time, Sylvia," suggested one friend.

Another chimed in, "Or give back the Christmas star."

Sylvia looked sharply at Claudia. She was not sure what astonished her more: that Claudia had blabbed to her friends about a family matter, or that she still blamed Sylvia for the disappearance of the star. "I don't have it," she said, the warmth and fellowship inspired by the Christmas worship slowly ebbing.

"I don't want to talk about that here." Claudia yanked Sylvia free of her choir robe, bundled it up, and dumped it into her sister's arms. "Give this back to Miss Rosemary. The other altos are already gone."

Biting back a retort, Sylvia did as Claudia commanded, shutting her ears to the older girls' laughter.

Great-Aunt Lucinda waited until every member of the family had returned home from church before unlocking the ballroom. Children rushed past her through the open door like water through a floodgate, and their shouts and squeals of delight upon discovering presents beneath the tree were deafening. Santa had come. Sylvia watched the children race from one gift to another searching for their names, seeing in their faces the utter happiness and delight that only a visit from Santa could bring. She missed feeling so captivated by wonder, swept up in the magic of Christmas, a magic that had once seemed as real as every other Bergstrom tradition. She smiled wistfully as she watched the younger children, wishing that just for Christmas morning she could be their age again — believing, trusting, not knowing everything she knew now. Still, it was such a joy to witness her brother and cousins enjoying a moment of complete happiness that she felt a surge of love for each of them, and a joy that in its own way was as magical and as full of wonder as what the children felt.

In the midst of all the clamor and excitement, Andrew sat on the floor, an island of stillness. He was so close to the tree that he was almost concealed within the branches, his eyes full of astonishment as he clutched two gifts, each with his name written in elegant script upon it.

"Don't open them yet," warned Richard, although Andrew clung to the boxes so tightly Sylvia doubted he could be compelled to set one down so he could open the other. "We have to eat breakfast first."

"That's right, children," called Great-Aunt Lucinda, clapping her hands for their attention. "Breakfast, then gifts. You know the rules."

A great moan of despair went up from the children, but then they remembered their hunger and raced off to the dining room. They gobbled their breakfast — eggs and sausage and apple strudel — and dashed back to the Christmas tree, unable to stay away from Santa's bounty for one moment longer than necessary. The older Bergstroms ate more leisurely, knowing that the older children would remind the younger that they were not allowed to open their gifts until everyone had finished breakfast.

"We should take our plates in there instead of taking our time and torturing them like this," remarked Uncle William, as he did every year. Everyone murmured assent and continued eating at their same, leisurely pace.

"The strudel is delicious, girls," said

Aunt Nellie, who had watched her mother-in-law make strudel once and had vowed never to learn the recipe.

"It is," agreed Sylvia's father, smiling warmly at his daughters. "I'm proud to see that you're carrying on the Bergstrom tradition. Your mother would have been proud of you two."

Sylvia smiled and was about to thank him for the compliment when Uncle William added, "With a few more years' practice, folks might not be able to tell the difference between your strudel and those of the more experienced bakers in the family."

"And even we are no match for Gerda," remarked Great-Aunt Lucinda. "She could make the lightest, flakiest pastry so effortlessly it could make you cry. I think that's why I always preferred to bake Christmas cookies. I couldn't help feeling like a failure when I compared my strudel to hers, so I gave up trying. Don't follow my poor example, girls. Stick with it and you might find that one of you has inherited Gerda's gift for pastry."

Sylvia caught her sister's eye and they shared a long look of commiseration. No Bergstrom girl escaped comparison to Gerda, and they were overdue for their turn. Sylvia cheered up when she thought of how much their second attempt to stretch the dough had improved upon their first. Next year, they would do even better. Judging by the few crumbs left on the plate where their strudel had been, their first attempt had been a success despite its flaws. The pastry was chewy where it should have been light and flaky, but the apple filling was as delicious as any Sylvia had tasted.

She would have taken more pleasure in the famous Bergstrom strudel had the Christmas star awaited them on the kitchen table. Though none of the adults mentioned the star at breakfast and Sylvia suspected most of the children had forgotten that it was still missing, she knew the prankster's disregard for her father's offer of amnesty troubled all of them.

Any hope that the prankster might have had a last-minute change of heart vanished as Sylvia helped Lucinda carry dirty dishes from the dining room to the kitchen. Only the jolly Santa Claus cookie jar and six red-and-green tartan placemats sat on the long wooden table.

"What will we put on the top of the tree?" Sylvia asked her great-aunt as they washed and dried the dishes, side by side.

"I don't know. We've used that star as

long as I can remember." Great-Aunt Lucinda shrugged. "Perhaps we'll just leave it bare and let the emptiness prick the conscience."

"You don't think I still have the star, do you?"

"No, Sylvia. I saw your face when you searched the empty crate and I know you were as bewildered as the rest of us."

"Then who?"

Lucinda was silent for a moment. "I have my suspicions, but I'll keep my own counsel."

Sylvia did not pester her, for she was suddenly taken by suspicions of her own. Who had been most eager to lay blame? Who had the most reason to want Sylvia's first attempt to hide the star fail?

Claudia.

"Aren't you coming?" called Richard, racing into the kitchen. "Everyone's waiting."

"I suppose the dishes won't get any dirtier if we save them for later." Smiling, Great-Aunt Lucinda shook soapsuds from her fingers and dried her hands on Sylvia's dishtowel. Richard whooped in delight and ran off to the ballroom where the other children were waiting eagerly with their gifts. Sylvia wished everyone could tear into their gifts all at once, as some of her friends' families did, but the Bergstroms took turns opening one gift at a time, proceeding in order from youngest to eldest. Sylvia received a beautiful cardigan Great-Aunt Lucinda had knit from the softest wool, a coordinating skirt from Claudia, W. B. Yeats's *Collected Poems* from her father, and from her brother, an illustrated story of a stagecoach robbery in the Wild West starring thinly fictionalized versions of the Bergstrom children.

The story Richard had written for Andrew was a slightly different version featuring the two boys. Andrew seemed pleased by his friend's gift, but he could hardly take his eyes off what Santa had brought him: a steel train set with an engine, two boxcars, a passenger car, and a bright red caboose. His expression, utter delight mixed with disbelief, touched and amused Sylvia. She suspected it was the nicest gift he had ever received. Suddenly she thought of his little sister and wondered what, if anything, she had found upon waking that Christmas morning. She had a horrible thought: How would that little girl feel when Andrew came home with beautiful new toys from Santa when she had received nothing?

She would think Santa had forgotten her.

How old was Andrew's sister — four? Five? Four, Sylvia decided. She looked younger, but Andrew, too, was small for his age. She was just about the age to enjoy — Sylvia looked around the room and her gaze fell upon Uncle William's youngest daughter, who was cradling the rag doll Santa had brought her. A doll. Of course. But Claudia's old dolls were too worn and faded from so many years of hard love, though they remained in the nursery for the cousins' visits. Sylvia had never cared for dolls, so she had none to give away.

Except —

Then she remembered a gift from her grandmother Lockwood, her mother's mother. The children had never met her until the day she came to live at Elm Creek Manor a few months before her death. When she first arrived, she had given Claudia an heirloom silver locket containing a picture of their great-grandparents that her own mother had given to her long ago. To Sylvia she gave a fine porcelain doll with ringlets of golden hair, dressed in a gown of blue velvet. It was a beautiful doll, but Sylvia had always preferred to play with toy horses and hardly knew what to do with it. But she had sense enough, even at eight years old, to hug the doll and pretend she liked the gift to show respect to the grandmother she barely knew.

Her grandmother had explained that the doll once belonged to Eleanor. "They were inseparable until she decided she was too old for dolls," said Grandmother Lockwood in a voice as dry and as crisp as a cracker. "Then she sat on a shelf in the nursery gathering dust, the poor, neglected thing."

"I didn't neglect it," Sylvia's mother had said, her voice carrying a hint of sharpness. "You're thinking of Abigail. That was her doll, not mine."

"That's not so," said Grandmother Lockwood. "I recall very clearly giving it to you for Christmas when you were four."

"That was Abigail. She said Santa brought it. When Abigail no longer wanted her, she gave her to me, but by then I was no longer interested in dolls, either."

"You would have liked them still if Abigail had." Grandmother Lockwood turned a sharp eye upon Sylvia. "Well, my dear, it seems I've given you the doll no one wanted. I suppose you, too, will abandon her."

Sylvia did not like the dismissive tone her grandmother used to address her mother, but she nodded gravely and promised she would never abandon the beautiful doll. She had kept her promise, although she had not showered the toy with the affection Grandmother had likely hoped to inspire.

The beautiful doll had once been a Christmas gift, and it had already been handed down twice. It would not be parting with a family heirloom to pass it on to a deserving little girl.

Sylvia slipped away from the party and dashed upstairs to her bedroom, where she stood on a chair on tiptoe to reach to the back of the top shelf where the box had sat untouched for years. She pulled down the heavy white cardboard box, blew off the dust, and removed the lid. The doll was as lovely as the day Sylvia had put her away, her blue velvet frock and white pinafore spotless, her golden curls perfectly arranged. When Sylvia picked her up, the blue eyes opened above the button nose and rosebud mouth. For a moment she considered giving it to her favorite little cousin, who still enjoyed dolls and would adore this one. But she had so many dolls — she had received a new one just hours ago — and so many other toys as well. Resolved, Sylvia tucked the doll carefully into the box and replaced the lid, then wrapped it and tied it with ribbon.

The children were distracted with their toys when she returned, and the other women were off in the kitchen seeing to Christmas dinner. When her father and the other men were not watching, Sylvia slipped the box unnoticed beneath the tree, then strolled away and waited for someone to notice the new gift. After a while, when no one did, Sylvia pointed to it and exclaimed, "Isn't that another present? How did we miss it?"

Her father gave her a speculative look as the children hurried to the tree and discovered the unexpected gift. "That wasn't there before," said Richard.

"Are you sure?" asked Sylvia. "Santa couldn't have returned while we were here. We would have seen him."

Richard threw her a brief, quizzical frown, but Andrew quickly drew his attention. "Sally Jane," he read. "That's my sister's name."

"We don't have a Sally Jane in the Bergstrom family," said Sylvia's father. "It must be for your sister. I wonder why Santa left it here."

"Maybe he made a mistake," piped up one of the cousins.

"Maybe he wants me to take it to her," said Andrew slowly. "I don't think he knows where we live now."

A shadow of concern passed over Sylvia's father's face. "I'm sure that's what Santa intended," he said. "He knows you're a responsible boy and that he can trust you to get this to your sister safely."

"I will," said Andrew solemnly. Then he smiled, and for a moment, Sylvia glimpsed a boy as happy and as certain that he was loved as her own dear Richard.

The rest of the day passed happily but all too soon. The children played with one another's new toys while the adults spoke of Christmases past and read aloud from the letters of absent loved ones. Cousin Elizabeth and her husband, Henry, had sent a whole box of oranges from their ranch in California. Great-Aunt Lucinda read Elizabeth's letter aloud so they could all enjoy her amusing stories about going to the beach in November and thinking of the folks back in Pennsylvania shivering by the fire, glimpsing a genuine movie star in a theatre — in the audience, not on the screen — and of her exasperation when, just after she had wiped away a blanket of dust that had settled throughout the house after a minor earthquake, an aftershock came along and threw another layer down. Sylvia shivered with excitement imagining her brave cousin pacing impatiently and waiting for an earthquake to stop, worried only about the mess she would have to clean up and completely indifferent to the danger.

Then Elizabeth's tone grew wistful. "I do miss Elm Creek Manor and all who reside therein, especially at this time of year," Great-Aunt Lucinda read. "I wish I could spend just one more Christmas surrounded by family. I make the famous Bergstrom strudel here, but it just isn't the same without the aunts and uncles there to tell me mine doesn't taste as good as Grandma Gerda's. On Christmas Eve, know that I will be thinking of you all and wondering which lucky child placed the star upon the tree that night." Great-Aunt Lucinda cleared her throat. "Good-bye for now and God Bless. Merry Christmas from your loving Elizabeth."

Sylvia ached to see her cousin again. She would even be glad to see Henry if only he would bring her beloved cousin home.

Christmas dinner was delicious. They had scrimped and saved for months so that they might have a feast that day, just as the first Bergstroms who had settled in that country had done. They savored the tender jagerschnitzel — grilled pork loin with mushroom gravy — sweet potatoes, creamed peas, and all the dishes without which Christmas would not seem complete. After the children were excused, the older members of the family lingered at the table, sharing Christmas memories and hopes for the year to come. The Depression couldn't last forever, Uncle William said, as he had the previous year. Better times were sure to come. The horses were thriving, and the Bergstroms would be ready when their old customers returned. In the meantime, the Bergstroms would weather the storm as they always had.

"What was in the box you gave to Andrew's sister?" Sylvia's father asked her.

"A doll," she replied. "She's like new. I rarely played with her."

"I can't remember ever seeing you with a doll," remarked Aunt Nellie. "It must have been very long ago."

Claudia leveled her gaze at her sister. "You don't mean Grandmother Lockwood's doll, do you?"

"Yes, that's the one."

"But she was Mama's!"

"No, she wasn't. She was Aunt Abigail's."

"But after that she was Mama's."

"Mama never played with her, and neither did I." Sylvia looked from her sister to her father, worried. "I thought Andrew's little sister would like to have her."

"It's a generous gift," said Great-Aunt Lucinda. "I'm sure little Sally Jane will adore her."

Claudia looked shocked. "You don't mean to let her go through with it?"

Great-Aunt Lucinda shrugged. "We can hardly take it back now."

Sylvia's father regarded Claudia, concerned. "Did you want the doll for yourself? Aren't you a little old for dolls?"

"I don't want it to play with. It's a family heirloom."

"You never showed any interest in it before."

Sylvia detected the trace of irritation in her father's voice and wondered if her sister did, too.

Indignant, Claudia replied, "I never dreamed Sylvia would give it away or I would have."

"What's done is done," said their father firmly. "It's a fine doll — for all that I know about dolls — but it was never a cherished family heirloom. Aunt Abigail played with it as a child but your mother never did, and even if she had, she would have been the first to offer it up to a little girl who hasn't had a tiny fraction of the blessings you children have received every day of your lives, Depression or no Depression. Your mother was generous that way, and it seems that Sylvia has learned from her. And for that, I am grateful."

Shocked, Sylvia could only stare at her plate, her face hot. She had never heard anyone speak so sternly to Claudia. In a strangled voice, her sister asked if she could be excused. Their father dismissed her with a nod, and she hurried from the dining room as quickly as she could without running.

"Nephew," chided Great-Aunt Lucinda after she had gone.

"I'm sorry, Aunt, but I just couldn't bear any selfishness today. Not on Christmas. Eleanor would have been so disappointed. And as for you, young lady —"

Sylvia quickly looked up. "Yes, Father?"

"You could have asked your sister first before giving away the doll." He held up a hand to stave off her protest. "I realize she never played with it, but you know how she loves the stories your mother used to tell about her life in New York. This doll is a link to the world she knows only through your mother's stories. Even so, I think she would have gladly given it to Andrew's sister if you had allowed her to have a say in the decision."

Ashamed, Sylvia lowered her eyes again. "I — I should have thought of that."

"Well, give her back the Christmas star and I'm sure she'll forgive you." Great-Aunt Lucinda laughed at Sylvia's expression. "I'm teasing, dear."

Sylvia's father glanced out the window. Although they had dined early, already it was dusk. "I suppose I'd better take Andrew home," he said, pushing back his chair.

The rest of the family saw them off, except for Claudia, who had not been seen since she left the supper table. Andrew seemed reluctant to go until Sylvia's father made a joke about how the car was so full of gifts that it reminded him of Santa's sleigh. The boy brightened at the idea and willingly climbed into the front seat beside Sylvia's father.

After they departed, Sylvia helped Aunt Nellie and Great-Aunt Lucinda tidy up the kitchen and dining room. They had almost finished when they heard her father return, opening the back door and stomping his feet on the steps to knock the snow from his boots before coming inside. Sylvia was putting away the dry dishes, but she heard her father talking to Lucinda at the back entry.

"We should have invited the whole family," he said, removing his coat. "I don't think they had much of a celebration."

"No Christmas dinner?" said Great-Aunt Lucinda.

"I'm not sure they had any dinner at all. Aunt, if you could see the squalor they live in —" He sighed, frustrated. "No man should have to raise his children that way. What is wrong with our country that we allow this to happen?"

"I don't know that our country is to blame."

"We *are* the country, Aunt. People like us. We all have to do what we can to help one another, just as my Eleanor said. But so many men out of work for so many years — That's not a problem that will resolve itself. Something must be done."

Fondly, Great-Aunt Lucinda teased, "Why, Frederick, are you asking for a Christmas miracle?"

"If there were any chance of getting one,

you'd better believe I'd ask." He fell silent for a moment. "Do you know what the boy said to me as I drove him home? He said that this was the best Christmas he had ever known. You and I, William and Nellie — and perhaps even the older children — we've compared these past few Christmases to those of the twenties and note how we've come down in the world, and yet this little boy was overwhelmed by our abundance."

"That's a lesson for us all."

"Aunt Lucinda —" He hesitated. "I can't help thinking how much more we could do for Andrew and his little sister if —"

"No, Frederick. I know your heart's in the right place, but you can't take children from their parents."

"If you could see their home, you'd feel differently."

"Perhaps, but that doesn't change the fact that there is much more to a home than material comforts."

"I'm not so sure that Andrew's home has all those intangibles."

"And I can't say for certain whether you're condemning them simply because they're poor. Nephew, dear, there are so many families like the Coopers. Are you going to take in all their children?"

"No," he said. "No, I suppose that would be impossible. But I can help this child and his sister."

"We will continue to share what we have with Andrew, just as we always have." Great-Aunt Lucinda sighed. "We should have thought of the little girl. Thank goodness for Sylvia's generous heart. We can and we should do more for Sally Jane, but at least today, she learned that Santa has not forgotten her."

Sylvia's father and great-aunt walked off down the hall, their conversation fading until Sylvia could no longer hear them. Was it true, as Great-Aunt Lucinda had said, that she had a generous heart? No one had ever said such a thing before, and she had never thought of herself that way. She just couldn't bear the thought of a little sister believing she was less loved than an older sibling. Santa couldn't remember Andrew and not Sally Jane. It simply would not be fair.

Christmas of 1934 was drawing to a close. Sylvia helped see the children off to bed, then curled up in a chair in the ballroom with the book of poems her father had given her, reading and enjoying the beauty of the lights on the Christmas tree, which seemed unfinished without the ruby-and-gold star on the highest bough.

She remembered then that she had not seen Claudia in hours. Marking her place in the book with a scrap of ribbon from a Christmas gift, she set it aside and went looking for her sister. She eventually found her kneeling on the floor of the front parlor, packing the Feathered Stars, appliquéd holly plumes, and haphazard Variable Stars into a box. Inside, Sylvia spotted the larger cuts of fabric from which Lucinda, Eleanor, and Claudia had taken the pieces for their blocks.

"Christmas is over, so you're putting the Christmas Quilt away?" asked Sylvia, amused in spite of herself. "I see you're following in Great-Aunt Lucinda's footsteps."

"Exactly," said Claudia shortly. "To the letter."

"What do you mean?"

"I mean I'm quitting, too. I suppose that pleases you."

Strangely, it did not please Sylvia at all. "Why quit when you've already made five blocks?"

"Because I've already wasted too much time on this wretched thing." Claudia closed the box and rose, then stood there with the box at her feet, regarding her sister challengingly, as if daring her to continue the conversation.

"Maybe you'll feel differently next Christmas," said Sylvia. "Maybe that's how you'll follow Great-Aunt Lucinda's example, by working on it only during the Christmas season."

"I will never sew another stitch of this quilt," Claudia vowed. "I don't want anything to remind me of this miserable Christmas."

Sylvia stared at her, bewildered. "What are you talking about?"

"Oh, for heaven's sake, Sylvia, don't pretend you don't know. It isn't like you to sympathize with me and I'm not fooled. This Christmas has been a disaster from start to finish, from the moment the strudel dough turned rubbery until ten minutes ago when I tried to sew two of my Variable Stars together and couldn't get the points to match. I used the exact same templates and measured each before I cut, and yet it still would not come together properly."

The trouble was her seam allowances, not her templates, Sylvia thought, but she decided to wait for a better moment to mention it. "The strudel was fine, and the proof is that only crumbs were left. And one bad quilt block isn't a disaster."

"It's not just that. It's everything."

Sylvia knew she was thinking of the missing Christmas tree star, Aunt Abigail's doll, Sylvia's embarrassing show of affection in the choir loft — everything. Or nearly so. Apparently she had forgotten the beautiful Christmas tree alight with candles, Great-Aunt Lucinda's delicious Christ- mas dinner, the sublime joy of the church service, the unbridled happiness of the children, and the loving company of their aunts and uncles and father. How could any of that be branded a disaster?

"When Father took Andrew home," said Sylvia, "the little boy told him that this was the most wonderful Christmas he had ever known."

Claudia looked away. "Well, of course it would be, for him."

Sylvia wanted to argue that it had been so, not only for Andrew, but for all of them, but she ached with longing for her mother and could not honestly say that any Christmas was as full of joy and hope as those Eleanor had shared with them. Of course that could not be so. But this Christmas had been full of blessings, and she could not understand why her sister could not see them.

* * *

Great-Aunt Lucinda was certain the ruby-and-gold glass star would be discovered when the family put away the trappings of the holiday after Twelfth Night, but it was not. Sylvia never saw the star again, and she doubted Claudia ever stopped suspecting she played a role in its disappearance.

In the year that was to come, Sylvia's father discovered that his instinct to remove Andrew and Sally Jane from their unhappy home was justified. Richard and Andrew were eight years old when Andrew ran away from home and hid out for days in the wooden playhouse Sylvia's father had built for Richard near the stables and exercise rings. Richard smuggled blankets and food to his friend, but he inadvertently led Sylvia right to him one early autumn night when she woke to the sound of her brother creeping past her bedroom door. When Sylvia's father contacted the authorities, whatever they discovered about the Cooper home compelled them to take Andrew and Sally Jane from their parents the first day of their investigation. Sylvia's father immediately offered to take them in, but an aunt was found in Philadelphia, and while the local authorities respected Frederick Bergstrom, the law said that the children belonged with family.

Andrew and his sister were sent away to the city. For months after his sudden departure, Richard missed his friend and wrote him letters, but the Bergstroms did not know where to send them. For years thereafter, the Bergstroms counted Andrew and his little sister among those absent loved ones with whom they longed to spend Christmas once more.

And on every one of those Christmases, Sylvia hoped her sister would reflect upon that year and realize that it had truly been a joyous time despite the mishaps and misunderstandings, and that she would finish the Christmas Quilt, even with her well-intended but imperfect stitches. If Claudia ever did see the Christmas of 1934 in a different light, she never shared that epiphany with her sister, nor did she ever add another stitch to the Christmas Quilt.

Chapter Four

Sylvia kept Sarah company in the sitting room as she finished attaching Claudia's Variable Stars to the Feathered Stars and holly plumes. As the disparate sections of the Christmas Quilt came together, Sylvia began to see a pattern emerging, but whether Sarah would succeed in creating something harmonious and beautiful, Sylvia could not yet determine.

The sight of Claudia's handiwork intermingled with their mother's and great-aunt's gave her mixed feelings. While Claudia's piecing skills were inferior to those of her predecessors, her pattern choice simpler, Sarah had arranged the Variable Stars so that they set off the complexity of the other blocks without competing for the observer's attention. They seemed to fit with an ease that made Sylvia question her reaction to her sister's pattern choice so many years before. Perhaps Sarah had not chanced upon a flattering arrangement. Perhaps this layout was what

Claudia had intended all along.

It remained to be seen how Sarah would accommodate the blocks Sylvia had made, or whether a Bergstrom sister would be excluded from the quilt after all — just not the sister Sylvia would have predicted.

In a moment when the clattering of the sewing machine had paused, Sylvia asked, "Would you care to help me finish putting up the Christmas decorations?"

"When I finish this section," Sarah promised, winding a new bobbin. "I'll meet you in the foyer, okay?"

Sylvia shrugged and left her to it. She returned to the boxes of Christmas decorations scattered across the marble foyer, and she cast a critical eye upon the work they had already completed. She made a few changes, made a mental note to have Matt collect some greenery, and, in armfuls she could manage, brought the rest of the decorations to the kitchen. On one of her trips, she discovered that the sewing machine had fallen silent, and that Sarah and Matt were discussing something in hushed voices within the sitting room.

She considered eavesdropping, but reminded herself that she rarely learned anything pleasant that way. So she went to the doorway and regarded the pair, who were speaking earnestly, their heads bent close together. She caught a few words — "mother," "impossible," and "never" — just enough for her to identify the topic of conversation.

"I hate to interrupt," she said, hiding a smile when they sat up too quickly. "But if we're going to finish decorating, I'll need your help."

"You're not interrupting anything," said Matt.

"We were just debating . . . which Christmas carol is the most depressing," said Sarah. "Matt says 'I'll Be Home for Christmas' because it's about longing for home rather than actually being there, but I think 'Have Yourself a Merry Little Christmas' is more melancholy. What do you think?"

"What an odd way to pass the time." Sylvia didn't believe her for a moment, but she decided to play along. "My vote goes to the 'Coventry Carol.' "

"Which one is that?"

"It's a traditional piece." Sylvia hummed a few measures. "It's about King Herod's slaughter of the innocents in his attempt to kill the Christ Child."

"You win," said Matt.

"Naturally. I have experience and

wisdom on my side." Not to mention years of practice debating Claudia on every conceivable topic. "Now then. If Sarah is willing to take a break from her sewing, I believe it's time you two went out and found us a tree."

Sarah and Matt agreed, so Sylvia reminded them of the borders of the Bergstrom estate, which had contracted significantly since her youth due to Claudia's sale of parcels of land in Sylvia's absence. She described a particular region of the woods that had yielded many fine Christmas trees in the past, advised them to take the old toboggan along, and sent them on their way.

Sylvia watched from the back stairs as they trudged off across the parking lot — empty of cars in the off-season, although Matt kept it cleared of snow in case of unexpected visitors — and crossed the bridge over Elm Creek. So many other couples had made that trek before them. It was a tradition that had begun with Hans and Anneke Bergstrom, as they went off to find a tree while Gerda, the superior cook, remained at home to attend to their Christmas Eve supper. Their simple, practical decision became ritual as younger generations married and the family grew. Once

Sylvia's parents had been the newlyweds sent off to find the Christmas tree, their love steadfast and hopes for the future bright despite the doctors' grim prediction that Eleanor's health would not allow her to bear children. Years later, their daughter Sylvia set off for the snowy wood with her beloved husband, James.

Dear, wonderful James.

They met at the state fair when Sylvia was sixteen. Every year she and Claudia entered their quilts in the show in hopes of winning a ribbon, and Great-Aunt Lucinda entered her best preserves. Their father showed his prize horses and spent hours debating the merits of various breeding and training practices with other men in the business, some of whom were his rivals. Nine-year-old Richard shadowed his father, absorbing every word the men exchanged. Like Sylvia, he had always known that one day he would take his place beside his father and uncle with Bergstrom Thoroughbreds.

Although Sylvia cared as much about the business as her brother, at the fair, she was too absorbed in her riding competitions to pay much attention to business trends and competitors' rivalries. She took first place in nearly every competition she entered, which she attributed as much to her father's fine horses as to her own skill. When she saw her father beaming at her proudly as the judges awarded her ribbons and draped a wreath of flowers around her mount's neck, she knew she was doing her part to strengthen the reputation of Bergstrom Thoroughbreds. After years of struggling, the family business was steadily regaining its former prominence. Recent outstanding showings in the Preakness had brought them new customers, and just as Uncle William had always predicted, many of their former clients had returned when they could afford to once again.

That year at the fair, a young man she did not recognize came often to the practice ring and leaned against the fence to watch while Sylvia rode Dresden Rose. Once, when he caught her eye and called out a greeting, she replied with a nod and pretended to ignore him. She had come to find his presence disconcerting and wondered if a rival had sent him to ruin her concentration and leave her vulnerable to mistakes in the ring. With dismay she realized that the plan, if it was a plan, had a good chance of succeeding. The young man was undeniably handsome, tall and strong with dark eyes and dark, curly hair, impossible to ignore.

Later, as she tended to Dresden Rose, the young man from the practice ring joined her in the stable. He complimented the mare, which he immediately recognized as a Bergstrom Thoroughbred, and inquired if Sylvia often rode their horses.

"Of course," said Sylvia.

"They're supposed to be the finest horses around."

"A lot of people think so."

He smiled. "I know I shouldn't admit this, but the best of my family's stable can't match the worst of Old Bergstrom's."

"Oh, really?" Sylvia was so astonished she nearly laughed. "I suppose 'Old Bergstrom' would be delighted to hear that."

"I bet he already knows." The young man went on to confide that his father intended to catch up to Old Bergstrom in a generation, but that he did not believe his father would succeed. One day, however, he himself would breed horses even finer than the best Old Bergstrom had to offer.

After that admission, when he asked for her name, Sylvia thought it prudent to offer only her first. When he introduced himself, she was startled to learn he was James Compson, the youngest son of her father's strongest rival.

James did not discover who Sylvia's father was until her next riding competition later that day. From atop Dresden Rose, she spotted her family cheering in the spectators' seats and waved to them, her confidence bolstered. Then, as she looked away into another part of the stands, her eyes met James's. His gaze was so steady and intense that the encouraging grin he offered completely unsettled her. She looked away and fought to compose herself as the announcer called out the names of the riders.

When it was her turn, the announcer's voice rang out so that all could hear. "Our fifth competitor — Sylvia Bergstrom!"

As Dresden Rose trotted into the ring, Sylvia risked a glance at James Compson and was pleased to see him staring at her with an expression of shock, bewilderment, and chagrin. Later, when he did not reappear at the practice ring, she regretted having fun at his expense. She should have told him who she was the moment he identified Dresden Rose as coming from her father's stables. Surely he did not believe she had run to her father with his idle talk about his father's plans — although part of her felt disloyal for not divulging what she knew.

James must have forgiven her, for the next time they met a few years later, he was as warm and friendly as ever. They struck up a correspondence that lasted several years as their friendship blossomed into love. When Sylvia was twenty and James twenty-two, they married, and James joined the Bergstrom family and the family business at Elm Creek Manor.

Their first Christmas as husband and wife marked a time of renewed hope and happiness in the Bergstrom household, which had grown smaller since the year Claudia had attempted to finish the Christmas Quilt. Great-Aunt Lucinda, the last child of Hans and Anneke Bergstrom, had passed away after a brief illness. Uncle William died after being thrown from a horse, and when Aunt Nellie remarried, she moved away with her children. Other cousins left the Elm Creek Valley, too, pursuing the promise of better jobs elsewhere when the family business faltered. Elm Creek Manor, which had once seemed so full and bustling with life, suddenly became unbearably large and empty to its few remaining residents. Though the threat of a war in Europe loomed on the horizon, James's arrival in the household promised that they had reached a turning point, that he would help the business to thrive, and that one day the manor would be restored to its former glory.

On their first Christmas Eve as husband and wife, Claudia hid her jealousy poorly as Sylvia and James pulled on their coats and boots in preparation for their snowy trek into the woods, but Sylvia gave her credit for trying. Claudia had known her beau, Harold, since high school and in all fairness should have been the first sister to marry, but Harold had yet to ask her. No one doubted that he would get around to it eventually, but it chafed Claudia that once again her younger sister had preceded her. "It's true you get to be first to bring in the tree," she had remarked as they made the famous Bergstrom strudel earlier that day. "But I will get to be the newlywed until Richard marries, which means I will have more turns than you."

Sylvia was in such good spirits that she had conceded Claudia's point and pretended to be annoyed that her term as the most recent bride might soon end. She did not mention that Harold did not seem to be in much of a hurry, and that if he didn't propose soon, Richard might very well be old enough to marry before Claudia did.

With the rest of the family wishing them

good luck from the back door, Sylvia and James headed out, stopping first at the barn for the ax, a coil of rope, and the toboggan. "Give you a ride?" James offered, inclining his head to the toboggan, his face lighting up with his smile.

"This is for the tree," Sylvia reminded him, placing a mittened hand close to his around the towrope.

A thick blanket of snow as soft as powder had fallen overnight, and though the sky was concealed behind thick clouds, the air was clear and still. They walked in a companionable silence until James stopped short at the base of a thin white pine. "How's this?"

"It's tall enough, but the branches are too sparse," replied Sylvia. "I like a fuller tree, don't you? The ballroom is so large, if we don't have a full tree, it disappears in the space."

"Then let's keep looking." James gave the rope a tug and they continued on. "In my parents' house, my father always wanted a floor-to-ceiling tree, but my mother preferred a small one to stand on a table top. She said that was the way her family had always done it, and to please her, my father went along with it. Over the years they collected too many ornaments to fit on one small tree, but instead of getting a larger one, they chose two small trees and kept them in different rooms. By the time I was in school, we had small trees on tabletops in almost every room of the house. When visitors came, my next-oldest sister and I would lead tours to make sure they didn't miss any of them."

Sylvia smiled at the image of her beloved husband as a boy on Christmas morning. "We could do that instead if you like, choose several little trees instead of one large."

"No, this is the Bergstrom home and we'll do it the Bergstrom way."

"This is the Compson home now, too." Sylvia linked her arm through his. "Compson children will be born here and live here. We must give Compson traditions their pride of place."

"Some Compson traditions," James conceded. "I will miss Christmas Eve church services and staying home Christmas morning, opening presents in my pajamas."

Sylvia laughed. "Maybe we could try that next year." She paused and gestured to a tree several paces to the left. "What about that one?"

James left the toboggan behind and

broke a trail through the snow. "It looks great, all right," he said, reaching out to touch the middle limbs. "It's full enough, but the branches are too slender. They won't hold much weight."

He demonstrated how easily they bent, and Sylvia could picture the whole tree slumping under the load of ornaments and garlands. "We need something sturdier," agreed Sylvia. "That's more important than its appearance, unless we want to be sweeping broken glass off the ballroom floor for the whole twelve days of Christmas."

They returned to the toboggan and ventured deeper into the stand of conifers. As they walked along, side by side, passing the stumps of past Christmas trees, Sylvia thought of all the Bergstrom women who had made this journey before her. Once they had been as young and hopeful and as full of love for their husbands as she.

"James," she said suddenly. "Promise me you'll never leave me."

"I promised you that when I married you."

"Promise me again."

He stopped and took both her hands in his, amused. "I, James Compson, promise you, Sylvia Bergstrom Compson, my lawfully wedded wife, that nothing on earth could compel me to leave you."

"Not even a war?"

He hesitated. "If we do get pulled into the war in Europe, I might not have a choice. You know that."

"Promise me you won't enlist. Wait until you're drafted. Promise me you'll go only if you have no other choice."

"You're asking me to make promises about something that might not happen." No trace of amusement remained in his face. "What if I have no choice but to enlist? What if it's my duty?"

"Make your duty be to me," Sylvia implored. "To this family. I lost two uncles to the Great War, and I know how my father's service haunts him. I don't want that for you. For us."

"Sylvia —"

"Please, James."

He fell silent, gathering up the rope to the toboggan. "All right," he said quietly. "I won't enlist unless it's what I have to do to protect you, to protect this family. What I ask in return is that you allow me to decide when that time has arrived."

She longed for him to correct his speech, to say that he had meant to say "if" instead of "when," but he did not. "Very well," she said. "Let us pray that time never comes."

He handed her part of the toboggan rope and they continued on.

Soon James halted and indicated a tree a few yards ahead. "How about that one?"

In amazement, Sylvia took in the blue spruce from trunk to highest bow. It was the most magnificent tree she had ever beheld. Their journey had taken them off the usual footpaths into a section of the Bergstrom woods she rarely visited, but still she wondered how she could have missed this tree before. Somehow, she thought, she should have known it was here.

"It's beautiful," she breathed. And it was — strong and full and tall. Perhaps too tall. "It looks about forty feet high."

"I would have guessed forty-five."

Sylvia smiled. "We'd never get that back to the house. We'd have to bend it in half to fit it in the ballroom, and even then it might still brush the ceiling."

James grinned, agreeing. "Pity, though. It's a beautiful tree."

"It's unfortunate we can't just lop off the top."

James studied the tree. "Who says we can't?"

"Common sense. You'd have to climb all that way carrying the ax, and then —"

James picked up the coil of rope, shouldered the ax, and headed for the base of the tree.

"James, no." Sylvia caught him by the sleeve of his coat. "Have you lost your mind? You could fall and break your neck."

"I've climbed a few trees in my day."

"But you're no lumberjack. Don't be foolish. There are other trees."

He placed a hand on a lower branch. "Not like this one."

Sylvia imagined the top of the tree crashing to the ground, her husband close behind. She pictured it falling the wrong way, pinning her beneath its weight. "We could both get very badly hurt; you do realize that, don't you?"

He brushed her cheek and grinned. "Sweetheart, have a little faith."

Sylvia threw up her hands and backed away. Even burdened by the rope and ax, James scaled the blue spruce with remarkable speed. Sylvia could not tear her eyes from him as he climbed, as if her line of sight held him aloft, and if she looked away for the barest instant, he would tumble to the ground. Soon only bits of his clothing were visible through the thick branches — the heel of his brown boot, the red wool scarf she had knit him.

Then she heard the chopping sound of metal biting wood and, minutes later, a shout of warning.

Instinctively she flung up an arm to shield her face as the top of the tree seemed to hang suspended in the air for a moment, before it tipped, deceptively slowly, and plummeted to the ground. A smaller shape followed.

Snowdrifts muffled the sound of two impacts.

Sylvia found that she was holding her breath, and that she had looked away. Frantically she searched the tree until she spotted James climbing down, the coil of rope upon his shoulder. The ax. He had tossed down the ax rather than carry it. The height, her worry — all had deceived her into misjudging the size of the second object to fall.

Sylvia ran to him and flung her arms around him just as his feet touched solid ground. "Never do that again, understand? You scared me half to death."

James regarded her, surprised. "I got you the perfect tree, didn't I?"

"You're more important to me than any tree."

"I'm glad to hear it."

Sylvia was still trembling, but she followed James to the fallen treetop and helped him raise it. It was undamaged, as full and perfectly shaped as it had seemed from far below. They loaded it on the toboggan and tied it down with the rope.

"We'll take this part back for everyone else to see," said James as they pulled the toboggan toward home. "We'll know what it really is — just a small part of something greater than anyone else can imagine."

"And the tree will keep growing," Sylvia added. They were not leaving only a stump behind. Their tree would continue to grow and if all went well, it would one day regain its former height. In twenty years, perhaps, they could return to the same tree — but surely they would no longer be the most recently married couple by then. If someone chose that tree again, it would have to be another pair of newlyweds passing on the Bergstrom traditions.

Together they pulled on the towrope and brought back their first Christmas tree to the family awaiting them inside in the warmth and light.

Sylvia and James chose the Bergstrom Christmas tree for three more seasons.

By their fourth Christmas as husband and wife, the anticipated additions to the family — a baby, Claudia's beau Harold — had not come, but otherwise the family's fortunes had prospered since their wedding day. Through the years, Richard's wanderlust had grown, and when he was sixteen, he finally persuaded their father to allow him to attend a young men's academy in Philadelphia. A few days after the term began, he wired home with the astonishing news that he had found Andrew and that they had resumed their close friendship. Sylvia was delighted that her brother had a friend at school, especially one who knew the city well, but she missed Richard terribly. Still, she usually kept her lonely worries to herself. It was the autumn of 1943, and with so many families losing brothers and sons every day, she had no right to complain when her brother was merely away at school.

That year she looked forward to Christmas with greater anticipation than ever before. On the day Richard was expected home for the school holidays, the manor buzzed with expectation and excitement. All day Sylvia paced around, taking care of last-minute preparations but rarely far from a window, looking out through the falling snow for her brother. Suddenly one of the cousins ran downstairs from the nursery shouting that a car was coming up the drive. Sylvia ran to the foyer, threw open the front door — and discovered that Richard had not come alone. She would not have minded if Andrew had accompanied him, but instead she found herself gaping at a small figure standing so shyly behind Richard that she might have been attempting to hide. The biggest blue eyes Sylvia had ever seen peered up at her from beneath a white fur hood, but nearly all of the rest of a small, pale face was hidden behind a thick woolen muffler.

Richard laughed, kissed his sister on the cheek, and guided his companion indoors.

That was how Sylvia met the love of her little brother's life.

Agnes Chevalier easily surpassed Claudia in beauty, her skin so fair and features so delicately perfect that she reminded Sylvia of a dark-haired version of the porcelain doll she had given to Andrew's sister years before. Aside from her loveliness, though, Sylvia concluded within hours of her arrival that it was impossible to understand what her brother saw in the girl. He must have lost his mind, because why else would he have brought her, without a chaperone, all the way from Philadelphia to disrupt the Bergstroms' Christmas? Didn't her own family want her?

Soon Sylvia discovered why they indeed might not, for as surely as she was the prettiest girl Sylvia had ever seen, she was also the silliest and most spoiled creature ever to set foot in Elm Creek Manor. Worst of all, Richard was obviously besotted with her and indulged her every whim. When she asked for coffee after supper just as Sylvia appeared with the tea service, Richard raced into the kitchen to put on the coffeepot. Even after Richard showed her the estate and explained to her about the business he would run someday, she still referred to the stable as a "barn" and a young horse as a "calf." At eleven o'clock on Christmas Eve, she came downstairs dressed for Midnight Mass — and without missing a beat, Richard escorted her to church even though all his life he had attended Christmas morning services like every other Bergstrom. At breakfast Christmas morning, she insisted that the legendary Gerda Bergstrom's strudel could not possibly taste as delicious as the one Sylvia and Claudia made, which was an entirely ridiculous assertion given that she had absolutely no proof one way or the other.

It irked Sylvia that her father seemed to

find the fifteen-year-old child charming, and that James and Claudia seemed unaware of the flaws that were so obvious to Sylvia. James even warned Sylvia that she had better get used to Agnes because she might become a permanent addition to the family. Sylvia shuddered at the very thought, but she resolved to conceal her feelings for Richard's sake. Surely time would prove Richard's interest to be nothing more than a passing fancy, and next Christmas, they would celebrate with just the Bergstrom clan again — and Harold, who always joined them. But that was fine with Sylvia, as he had been Claudia's beau so long he might as well be family.

Sylvia's prediction could not have been more wrong.

In the following spring, Richard responded to the increasing anti-German sentiment in the country by deciding to lie about his age and enlist to prove his patriotism and loyalty. His best friend, Andrew, planned to join up with him. Alerted to their intentions, James and Harold raced to Philadelphia, but arrived too late to stop them — too late as well to prevent Richard and Agnes from marrying. They were no different from so many other young couples faced with separation who married in haste, but Agnes's parents must have consented only reluctantly because she was no longer welcome in their home.

Richard and Andrew were given two weeks before they were due to report for basic training, so Richard accompanied his bride when James and Harold brought her back to Elm Creek Manor. It was only then that Sylvia learned that James and Harold had enlisted, too, because if they did so immediately they were promised that they could remain together.

"It was the only way, Sylvia," James insisted as she reeled from shock. "It was the only way. I'll look after him. I promise you that. I promise we'll all come home safe to you."

There was nothing she could do. He had enlisted; he could not take it back. Nor could she rage at him for breaking the promise he had made to her that Christmas Eve. He had enlisted in order to look after her beloved younger brother. He believed he was doing what was necessary to protect her, to protect their family.

The men's last days at Elm Creek Manor flew swiftly by. Harold asked Claudia to marry him, and she accepted. Sylvia half expected them to wed at the county courthouse before Harold departed, but Claudia said they would marry after he came home. Harold did not seem pleased by the delay, but he could hardly complain considering that it was his fault they had not married years earlier.

Before Sylvia could come to terms with the men's imminent departure, they left for eight weeks of basic training. Sylvia saw her husband one last time before he shipped out, spending more than she could reasonably afford on train fare and a boarding house because she could not bear to stay away. Though James was the only one of them granted overnight leave, she managed to see the other three men at the base before they shipped out. Richard and Andrew were proud and excited about their deployment, while Harold was reticent and wary and wore his fatigues uncomfortably. Only James seemed unchanged, the same beloved man but for the uniform.

She was not the only wife or sweetheart who had come to bid a lover farewell. When it was time to part, she stood behind a chain link fence with other women as the men marched back to their barracks, some shouting encouragement to the soldiers, others waving and promising to write, many weeping. Sylvia held the men in her sight as long as she could, wanting James and Richard's last glimpse of her to be a comfort to them while they were away. They needed to know she would be strong, that she would hold the family and the business together in their absence. She wanted their last memory of her to be a source of courage and pride.

But Harold ruined it. At the last moment, he sprinted back and linked his fingers with hers through the chain link fence. "Will you give Claudia a message?"

Sylvia nodded. "Of course. Anything."

"Will you ask her to wait for me?"

At first Sylvia was confused. "I thought she accepted your proposal."

"Yes, but —" He hesitated. "I may be gone a long time, and she's a beautiful girl . . ."

Sylvia's heart hardened. "My sister has loved you since she was seventeen years old," she snapped. "It's outrageous that you would doubt her loyalty now. You've had every opportunity to marry her. It's not her fault you squandered your time."

She turned from his startled, wounded face and strode away as quickly as she could. She did not turn around to see if James had witnessed the exchange, if his last memory of her would be of anger and spite.

Within weeks of the men's deployment, Sylvia discovered she was pregnant.

Months passed. Letters from the men were infrequent and cherished, though sometimes they were censored so thoroughly Sylvia could hardly make sense of them. Sylvia threw herself into sustaining her household, volunteering for the war effort however she could, organizing scrap metal drives, and buying war bonds — anything. She would have joined the WACs or moved to Pittsburgh and taken a job in one of the factories that had been turned over to war production if she had not been needed at home to manage Bergstrom Thoroughbreds. And if she had not thought it might endanger the baby.

She thanked God for the baby, for a piece of James she carried with her always. His child gave her hope, a future to look forward to. By late autumn, her morning sickness had eased, but no one looking at her would have guessed she was expecting. Claudia told her to count her blessings, but Sylvia longed for a round belly, proof that the child was real and alive and growing. Once, when the last brown leaves had fallen from the trees in the winds of early winter, Sylvia confided to her sister that she would be devastated if James did not return home in time to hold his newborn child. Claudia told her not to worry. She had heard on the radio that the Allies had made so many gains in Europe that the war would be over by Christmas. Sylvia prayed she was right.

December came, with no sign that the war would end soon. Sylvia devoted herself to managing the business and the household — and her young sister-in-law, who tested Sylvia's patience with her tearfulness and need for consolation. Sylvia feared for her husband and brother too, but she did not pace frantically on the veranda if the postman were late, or dissolve into sobs if a wistful romantic song played on the radio. She knew they had to be strong, to accept without complaint their hardships and loneliness. Nothing they faced at Elm Creek Manor could compare to what their men endured.

Sylvia would have thought a girl as anxious as Agnes would have avoided stories from the front lines, but she dragged Sylvia and Claudia to the theater in Waterford at least once a week to watch the newsreels. The tension in the audience mirrored Sylvia's own as scenes of battles flashed upon the screen; she scanned every soldier's face for James and Richard and Andrew — even Harold. She worried about his safety, too, for Claudia's sake. She had not passed on his last message to her sister. What good would it have done them? What he had meant as a profession of love seemed to question her fidelity. Sylvia thought it a kindness to forget he had ever spoken.

Watching the newsreels provided the Bergstrom women with an odd sort of comfort, allowing them a glimpse into their men's lives and, in knowing what they endured, helping to share their burden. Newsreels of other women's husbands and sweethearts sufficed when they had no word from their own. Letters were their lifeline, but weeks often passed between letters from the Pacific, then several would arrive at once, their dates often spanning several weeks.

If Claudia were in an especially pensive mood, she would skip the news and arrive only in time for the feature, but Agnes studied the newsreels as unflinchingly as Sylvia. Over time, Sylvia began to develop a grudging respect for the girl. She had stolen a peek at several of Agnes's letters to Richard, and was surprised to find not one word of complaint, only loving encouragement and amusing descriptions of how she spent her days. Agnes joined Sylvia in all of her volunteer activities, and although she couldn't sew to save her life, she could knit with impressive speed and never dropped a stitch. Although her clothes, her speech, and her general unfamiliarity with all things practical indicated that she had led a life of privilege before marrying Richard, she had somehow learned frugality along the way, for she darned socks and mended torn sweaters so well that her repairs were nearly invisible. If she came upon a garment that had been outgrown or could not be mended, she unraveled the stitches, wound the yarn into balls, and knit socks and washcloths for the Red Cross to give to soldiers.

Perhaps this was the side of Agnes that had won Richard's heart.

Two days before Christmas, Sylvia's longing for her husband became almost too much to endure. She sat in the front parlor with Claudia and Agnes, stroking her swelling abdomen and dreaming of James holding their baby. Claudia cut templates for her wedding quilt and mused about her gown, while Agnes's knitting needles provided accompaniment to "I'll

Be Home for Christmas" on the radio.

Sylvia couldn't bear it. "Turn that off," she ordered. Claudia paused in the middle of a description of possible bodice designs and stared at her. Sylvia hauled herself from her chair and snapped off the radio. "I can't listen to that anymore. They aren't coming home for Christmas, so what's the use of dreaming about it?"

"Sometimes dreams are all we have," said Agnes softly.

It was exactly the sort of thing Sylvia might have expected her to say. Sylvia needed more than dreams. She needed James beside her. She needed Richard home and safe.

"What we need is a Christmas miracle," said Claudia. "For the war to end. If ever we ought to pray for peace on earth, this is the time."

"The war will end when we win," said Sylvia tiredly. However long it takes, however many lives it takes.

They fell silent. Embarrassed by her outburst, Sylvia was about to turn the radio back on when Claudia spoke. "We haven't done anything to prepare for Christmas."

"We sent the boys their packages," said Agnes.

"Yes, but we've done nothing around

here." Claudia gathered up her quilt pieces and set them aside. "We should make cookies from some of Great-Aunt Lucinda's old recipes."

"We don't have enough sugar rations," Sylvia pointed out.

"Then at least we should decorate." Claudia rose and reached for Agnes's hand. "Come on. We need something to remind us of the joy and hope of the season. Let's get those boxes out of the attic. Not you, Sylvia. You shouldn't carry anything heavy in your condition. Sit and rest."

"I've been sitting and resting all day," Sylvia grumbled, but her interest had been kindled. When Claudia and Agnes did not immediately return with the decorations, she went to the kitchen and checked the pantry for flour, sugar, and spices. She already knew they had plenty of apples down in the cellar. The ample harvest that year had been a mixed blessing, for with the men away, their abundant crop had been too much for the four remaining Bergstroms to harvest on their own. Rather than allow the apples to rot on the ground, they took enough for themselves and sent word throughout the town that anyone willing to pick the apples was welcome to take away whatever he could carry. Friends and neighbors as well as townsfolk they scarcely knew accepted the offer, and some left gifts of surplus produce from their own gardens in trade. One sunny afternoon, an entire Boy Scout troop arrived and harvested bushel after bushel of the ripe fruit. Each boy took some home to his family, but most were delivered to hospitals and soup kitchens throughout the state. Many more were sent to VA hospitals or USO outfits, nourishing wounded soldiers as well as those who had not yet seen battle.

Apples the Bergstroms had in abundance, and they had enough of the remaining ingredients to spare for one strudel. Tomorrow, Sylvia resolved, she and Claudia would make one. Perhaps Agnes would like to learn.

She returned to the foyer just as Claudia and Agnes began unpacking the decorations. She joined them, stopping by the parlor first to open the door and turn on the radio so they could listen as they worked. A quiet happiness filled her as she unwrapped the familiar trappings of the holiday — Richard's soldier nutcracker, the paper angels she and Claudia had made in Sunday school, Great-Aunt Lucinda's Santa Claus cookie jar. They had never found the ruby-and-gold glass star for the top of the tree; the highest bough had remained bare every year since it went missing. Sylvia had been sorry to see the traditional search for the star go, but this year, there were no children in the house to hunt for it anyway — unless, she thought saucily, they counted Agnes.

"Look what I found," said Agnes, peering into a white cotton pillowcase, plumped full as if a lumpy pillow were inside. For a moment, Sylvia thought she had discovered the star, but the colorful pieces she took from the pillowcase were fabric, not glass. "Is this a quilt?"

A lump formed in Sylvia's throat and she looked to Claudia, who stood frozen in place. "Pieces of one, anyway," said Sylvia, when her sister did not reply.

Agnes laid the Feathered Star blocks on the marble floor. "These are lovely."

"Our great-aunt made them," said Claudia quietly. She resumed setting candles into brass holders on the windowsills.

Agnes reached into the pillowcase again. "This appliqué is lovely," she said, admiring the holly plumes. "If I thought I could make something so beautiful, I might be tempted to learn to quilt."

"It's not as easy as it looks," said Sylvia.

Agnes regarded her mildly. "I didn't say it looked easy."

"I could teach you to quilt," offered Claudia.

"No, thank you." Agnes gave the quilt blocks one last admiring look before returning them to the pillowcase. Sylvia was disappointed that Agnes had not emptied the makeshift bag. Claudia might not offer quilting lessons so freely after Agnes gave her opinion of those Variable Star blocks. "Why didn't your great-aunt finish?"

"She wasn't the only one to work on it," said Sylvia. "My mother did the appliqué, and Claudia pieced five other stars. They're probably still in the case if you want to look."

"Didn't you make anything for the quilt?"

"Why, no." Sylvia glanced at Claudia, who was feigning disinterest as she unpacked ornaments from the green trunk. "Claudia said she wanted to finish it herself, so I —"

"You may complete it if you like," said Claudia. "I have too much sewing for my wedding to spend time on another project. It was never that important to me anyway. I haven't touched it in ten years."

Sylvia knew she had not; Sylvia had not

seen one thread of the quilt since Claudia put the fragments away on that Christmas Day so long ago. How the pieces had ended up in a pillowcase in the trunk with the Christmas decorations, she had no idea.

Uncertain, Sylvia studied her sister. "You honestly wouldn't mind? You said you never wanted to see any part of this quilt again. You said you couldn't bear to be reminded of the worst Christmas ever."

Claudia laughed shortly. "I think we would all agree that *that* Christmas hardly deserves that title anymore."

"Don't say such things." Agnes rose, holding the pillowcase carefully, as if it contained something precious and fragile. "This may be a lonely Christmas, but it is still Christmas. Sylvia, I agree that you should finish the quilt. It will help put us all in the holiday spirit."

Agnes held out the pillowcase, and when it seemed that she would stand there with her arm outstretched forever unless Sylvia took it, she did so. "I couldn't possibly finish it by Christmas Day."

"I might not know how to quilt, but I do know that much." Agnes smiled and returned to the blue trunk. "Why not set yourself a goal of finishing it before next

Christmas so that you and James can play with the baby upon it beneath the Christmas tree?"

Sylvia's heart warmed at the image that played in her mind's eye. The Christmas tree, blooming with light and color. James, home and safe, beaming proudly at their child. Their precious son or daughter, with bright eyes, a rosebud mouth, sitting up or crawling — goodness, what would the baby be doing at this time next year? The Christmas Quilt, a soft comfort beneath them all.

Sylvia ached to begin, but she hesitated. "The decorations —"

"We can finish without you," Agnes assured her.

"You should be sitting with your feet up anyway," remarked Claudia, without looking up from her work.

Sylvia was about to retort that she wasn't an invalid, but she reconsidered. It was, after all, the perfect excuse. "I'll be in the sitting room," she said, and went off with the pillowcase in hand to find her sewing basket.

In her favorite room just off the kitchen, Sylvia spread out the blocks on the floor and studied them. The fabrics remarkably had not faded through the years; the colors were as bright and merry as the day Great-Aunt Lucinda chose them so long ago. The Feathered Star blocks and holly plumes were as lovely as she remembered, and since Claudia's Variable Stars used many of the same fabrics, it might be possible to scatter them among the finer handiwork so that their flaws would not be apparent. But what should Sylvia's contribution be? What could she add to help bring the disparate pieces together harmoniously?

Sylvia thought back to the Christmas when Lucinda had set aside the quilt for the last time in order to help with the sewing for cousin Elizabeth's wedding. The Bergstrom women had made Elizabeth a beautiful gown and a Double Wedding Ring bridal quilt embellished with floral appliqués. A few weeks before the wedding, little Sylvia found Great-Aunt Lucinda working on a new quilt, a pattern of concentric rectangles and squares, one half of the block light colors, the other dark. It resembled the Log Cabin block so closely that at first Sylvia mistakenly believed them to be practice blocks for her quilting lessons.

But Great-Aunt Lucinda told her that this was another quilt for cousin Elizabeth, a sturdy scrap quilt for everyday use, something to remember her great-aunt by. "This pattern is called Chimneys and Cornerstones," she explained. "Whenever Elizabeth sees it, she'll remember our home and all the people in it. We Bergstroms have been blessed to have a home filled with love from the chimneys to the cornerstone. This quilt will help Elizabeth take some of that love with her."

Sylvia nodded to show she understood. It did not matter that these were not Log Cabin blocks. The upcoming wedding had left her so morose that the further postponement of her quilting lessons had lost the power to disappoint her.

Great-Aunt Lucinda traced a diagonal row of red squares, from one corner of the block to the opposite. "Do you see these red squares? Each is a fire burning in the fireplace to warm Elizabeth after a weary journey home."

"You made too many," said Sylvia, counting. "We don't have so many fireplaces."

She laughed. "I know. It's just a fancy. Elizabeth will understand. But there's more to the story. Do you see how one half of the block is dark fabric, and the other is light? The dark half represents the sorrows in a life, and the light colors represent the joys."

"Then why don't you give her a quilt with all light fabric?"

"I suppose I could, but then she wouldn't be able to see the pattern. The design appears only if you have both dark and light fabric."

"But I don't want Elizabeth to have any sorrows."

"I don't either, love, but sorrows come to us all. But don't worry. Remember these?" Great-Aunt Lucinda touched several red squares in a row. "As long as these home fires keep burning, Elizabeth will always have more joys than sorrows."

The meaning of the quilt had comforted Sylvia as a child, and now, the memory of Great-Aunt Lucinda's love warmed her heart once again. Cousin Elizabeth had journeyed so far that none of the Bergstroms expected to see her again. God willing, Sylvia would see her husband and brother, and Andrew and Harold. Until then, the Bergstrom women would keep the home fires burning. They would keep a candle in the window to welcome their loved ones home.

And while they waited, Sylvia would stitch her joys and sorrows into the Christmas Quilt, using the fabrics of the women who had gone before her to make the Log

Cabin blocks she had never had the chance to make with her great-aunt.

She chose red scraps for the center of the Log Cabin blocks and sewed rectangles of evergreen and snowy white around them, alternating the colors so that one half of the block was light and the other dark, divided along the diagonal. Sometimes the greens were so dark they appeared almost black, and often an ivory or muslin scrap slipped in among the white. The variations added depth and dimension to her work, subtle nuances that enhanced the beauty of the clearer hues.

Lost in reminiscences of Christmases past and the Christmas future she yearned for, Sylvia passed the day in sewing and reflection. Later, when hunger beckoned her from the sitting room, she discovered her home transformed by the loving attention of her sister and sister-in-law. All the old familiar decorations adorned the foyer, the ballroom, the other nooks and corners where so many memories lingered. Candles glowed softly in the windows; wreaths of holly and ivy graced the doors.

"We need a tree," said Agnes as they prepared a simple dinner for themselves and Sylvia's father, who was in bed recovering from a bout of the flu and needed his meal brought up to him on a tray.

Claudia glanced out the window. The sun touched the horizon, and the elm trees along the creek cast long shadows that stretched across the snowy ground and brushed the manor as if longing to come inside into the warmth. "We can't look for a tree tonight," she said. "It's too late. It will be dark by the time we finish dinner."

"Tomorrow, then," said Agnes cheerfully. "That's the proper day, isn't it? Richard told me your family always chooses the tree on Christmas Eve."

Sylvia wondered what else Richard had told her.

After dinner, she returned to the sitting room to work on the quilt. Claudia and Agnes joined her, each tending to her own work, but not so absorbed that they did not pause from time to time to admire Sylvia's progress.

The next morning, Sylvia returned to the Log Cabin blocks after breakfast and sewed until Claudia suggested they make strudel. The sisters set Agnes to peeling apples while they mixed and kneaded the dough, then took up their paring knives to assist her while the dough rested.

"In Philadelphia, my parents employed a chef who had trained in Paris," Agnes said as they sliced the peeled apples into uniform pieces. "Every year he made the same dessert, a rolled cake decorated to resemble a yule log."

"Bûche de noël," said Sylvia, her mother's words suddenly rising to the forefront of her memory.

"Yes, that's what he called it." Agnes gave her a curious look. "Have you ever made one?"

"Never, but my mother's family served it every year when she was a child."

Agnes nodded thoughtfully, and Sylvia suddenly wondered what her mother would have thought of the young woman. They might have more in common than Sylvia had ever suspected.

When the apple filling was prepared and the dough had rested, Sylvia and Claudia demonstrated how to stretch it. Agnes was impressed, but too worried about ruining the dough to try her hand at it. Sylvia was willing to let her be, but Claudia would not tolerate such reluctance. "You're a Bergstrom woman, and Bergstrom women need to learn this recipe," she insisted. "Besides, Sylvia really ought to get off her feet and I can't finish on my own."

Sylvia knew her sister could manage perfectly well, but she said nothing because the fib finally convinced Agnes to roll up her sleeves and try. Standing opposite Claudia, she reached beneath the dough and pulled it toward her with the backs of her hands, mirroring her sister-in-law. At first her efforts were so timid that she made no difference at all, but with encouragement from Claudia and teasing from Sylvia, she grew bolder. The dough had nearly doubled in area when Agnes's wedding ring snagged on the dough, tearing it.

"You should have removed your jewelry first," said Sylvia, leaving her stool to help Claudia seal the gap.

"Never," said Agnes. She closed her right hand around her left fingers so fiercely that Sylvia and Claudia laughed. Agnes worked more carefully after that, but she still tore the dough twice more before it reached the edges of the table.

Before long the strudel was in the oven baking, filling the kitchen with the enticing aroma of apples and cinnamon. "It smells divine," said Agnes, inhaling deeply as she swept up apple peelings from the floor.

"It does," Claudia agreed, "but it doesn't smell half as wonderful as Gerda Bergstrom's did."

"How would you know?" demanded Sylvia.

Claudia looked at her, surprised. "I suppose I don't," she said. "I've heard it repeated so often I assumed it was true."

Sylvia laughed.

"Now that we've finished the strudel, should we set out to find a tree?" asked Agnes.

Sylvia's mirth vanished. "We can't leave the house while the strudel's baking. It might burn."

"We don't all have to go," said Claudia. "One of us could stay behind."

"It would take all our combined strength to bring in a tree," countered Sylvia. "You've never done it, so you don't know. It's a heavy load to haul on the toboggan, even with a strong man at your side."

Agnes shrugged. "So we'll pick a smaller tree. We can't have Christmas without a tree."

Sylvia thought back to the four Christmases of her marriage, to the four times she and James had ventured out into the woods to search for the perfect Christmas tree. None of the later searches had been as dramatic as the first, but each had been memorable in its own right. Each blessed them with a revelation about their marriage — how they worked together, made decisions, showed respect, disagreed —

some facet of their relationship that had been present all along, brought to the surface for them to accept with joy, or to resolve to change. After sharing so much with James every Christmas Eve of her married life, she could not bear to have anyone else take his place at her side, not even a sister.

"It is a Bergstrom family tradition that the most recently married couple chooses the tree," said Sylvia. "James is not here, I can't bring in a tree alone, and I don't want to go with anyone else. Rather than break family tradition, I've decided against having a tree this year."

Claudia peered at her. "So you believe that the most recently married couple, or bride, in this case, should decide whether we have a tree."

"Exactly."

"That sounds reasonable to me."

"Good," said Sylvia, surprised that her sister had conceded so easily.

With a triumphant grin, Claudia turned to Agnes. "It's up to you, then. Should we have a tree this year or not?"

Startled, Sylvia spun to face Agnes. She had forgotten. It was too cruel to admit, but it was sometimes difficult for her to remember that Richard was married, that

Agnes was more than a visitor.

"If it's up to me . . ." Agnes avoided Sylvia's eyes. "I would like to have a tree."

Claudia's smile broadened in satisfaction, sparking Sylvia's anger. "You'll have to bring it in yourselves," Sylvia said, and strode off to the sitting room to work on the Christmas Quilt.

She heard them at the back door dressing to go out into the snow, but she did not move from her chair. She worked on the Christmas Quilt, pausing only to take the strudel from the oven — baked to a perfect golden brown — and fix lunch for her father. She placed a bowl of soup, some crackers, and a mug of hot tea with lemon and honey on a tray and carried it up to the library, where her father was reading a book in an armchair in front of the fireplace, wrapped in a blue-and-white Ocean Waves quilt her mother had made long ago.

"Lunchtime," she announced. "Chicken noodle soup and tea with honey."

"Better than any medicine." Carrying his book and holding the quilt around himself, her father joined her at the large oak desk and seated himself in the leather chair as she placed the tray before him. "What are you girls up to down there? I thought I heard the back door open."

"Claudia and Agnes went out for a Christmas tree." Sylvia nudged a stack of business papers out of the way and moved the bowl of soup closer.

"Oh?" Her father brightened. "That's a fine idea. I was beginning to think you girls didn't want a tree this year."

"Agnes had her heart set on it."

"Do you need me to help place it in the stand?"

"We'll manage, Father. Thank you."

"Nonsense." A fit of hoarse coughing interrupted him. "I'm feeling fine."

"Oh, yes, I can see that you are. You should be in bed." At his warning look, she held up her palms. "Fine. You're on the mend. I'm not going to argue with you."

"You're the one who should be in bed," he pointed out, indicating her abdomen with a nod.

"Now *that* is nonsense," said Sylvia, dismissing his advice with a smile. "I'll let you know when the tree is in place so you can help decorate."

Not long after she returned to her quilt, she heard the back door open. A moment later, Claudia stood in the sitting room doorway, still in her coat and boots. "Sylvia," she said, fighting to catch her breath, "I need your help."

Alarmed, Sylvia hauled herself awkwardly to her feet. "What's wrong? Is Agnes hurt?"

"No, but she's — I can't explain. Just come with me."

Quickly Sylvia threw on some old winter clothes of James's, having outgrown her own coat, and followed her sister outside. They trudged through the snow toward the largest stand of evergreens, following the narrow trail Claudia and Agnes had broken earlier.

They had not ventured far. They were still within sight of the manor when Sylvia spotted Agnes's coat and hood through the bare-limbed elms on the other side of the creek. The young woman stood fixed in place, gazing up into the branches of a Frazier fir. It was full, tall, and straight, and as they drew closer, Sylvia could see why Agnes had chosen it.

"What's the matter?" Sylvia asked, lowering her voice. "Is she afraid to hurt herself with the ax? Do you need me to do it?"

"You're welcome to try, if she'll let you."

As they reached Agnes, Sylvia realized that the emotion in her sister's manner was exasperation, not worry. "Agnes?" she asked carefully. "Is something wrong with the tree?"

"No." Agnes stared up at it, her expression unreadable. "It's perfect."

Sylvia looked around for the ax and spotted it on the toboggan. "Then let's cut it down and take it inside."

"No!" Agnes caught Sylvia by the coat sleeve before she could lift the ax. "Don't you see? There's a bird's nest up there."

She pointed, and Sylvia followed the line of her finger to a spot just above the midsection of the tree. After a moment's scrutiny, she was able to discern a nest of twigs, brown leaves, and straw hidden within the spruce branches.

"I told her it's abandoned," said Claudia. "All the birds have flown south for the winter."

"Not all of them," countered Agnes. "Some chickadees don't. Neither do owls and woodpeckers."

"What sort of bird made that nest?" asked Sylvia.

Agnes hesitated. "I don't know."

"Then it most likely belonged to a robin who left for sunnier skies months ago." Claudia shook her head. "It's almost certain that's an uninhabited nest."

"*Almost* certain," said Agnes. "I don't

want to destroy the home of a living creature if we can't do any better than 'almost.' Even if the bird did migrate, what will it think when it returns home in the spring and discovers its home is gone?"

Sylvia had never given much thought to what birds thought, or even if they did. "Perhaps the bird would be glad to have the excuse to build a nice, new nest in a tree deeper in the woods."

Incredulous, Agnes looked at her. "Is that how you would feel? Is that how you think the boys would feel if they came home from the war and found that we had torn down Elm Creek Manor and moved into the old Nelson farmhouse because it was closer to town?"

Claudia threw up her hands. "This is so far beyond reasonable that I don't think the word has been invented yet to properly describe it."

Agnes, hurt and close to tears, turned her gaze back to the tree. Sylvia saw that she was biting the inside of her cheek to keep from crying.

"I have a solution," she said carefully. "Why don't you pick another tree, one without a nest in it?"

"No." The set of Agnes's jaw showed that she was resolute. "It has to be this one. I knew the moment I saw it."

"But —" Sylvia threw Claudia a helpless glance, but Claudia just shook her head. "We have so many trees, and you haven't spent much time looking. I'm sure you'll find another tree just as lovely."

"No, I won't. I didn't set out to find an adequate tree or the most convenient tree. I set out to find the right one, and I did. This is the one I choose. Haven't you ever found something and known in your heart that it was meant to be yours?"

Sylvia had, once. She sighed. "Well, you found it all right, but you can't keep it."

"I know that," said Agnes.

Sylvia thought for a moment. "We could move the nest to another tree."

"You are not climbing a tree in your condition," said Claudia. "Let Agnes do it."

"I don't know how to climb trees," said Agnes defensively. "One doesn't get much practice in a city."

"You know a lot about the migratory habits of the birds of Pennsylvania for a girl who's never climbed a tree."

"Stop bickering," ordered Sylvia. "I'm trying to think." Claudia was right to say Agnes was not being reasonable, but Sylvia had never seen the younger girl dig in her heels before, and she had to admit it was a change she approved of. She also sensed that something else lay beneath the surface of Agnes's insistence. Somehow the fate of the absent bird, their men overseas, and Agnes's own exile from her family home had become intertwined in the young woman's mind, and although Sylvia didn't quite understand it, she longed for a solution that would bring peace to Agnes's troubled heart and restore contentment to the family.

A light gust of wind stirred the trees, sending a light dusting of snow upon Agnes's fir. The tiny crystals glittered like diamonds in the midday sun.

Suddenly it came to her. "Let's decorate the tree out here."

The others stared at her, Claudia bewildered, Agnes hopeful. "Out here?" echoed Claudia.

"Yes, why not? It's within sight of the house. We can enjoy it from the ballroom windows."

Claudia was aghast. "Hang ornaments that have been in the family for generations on a tree outside in the dead of winter?"

"We don't have to," exclaimed Agnes. "We've already strung popcorn and cranberries and nuts. We can trim the trees with those —"

"And apples, for a bit of color," added Sylvia.

"And candles for the light —"

"Oh, yes, by all means," interrupted Claudia. "What's Christmas without a forest fire?"

"Very well, forget the candles." Agnes beamed at Sylvia. "Will you help me?"

Sylvia smiled. "Of course."

Once Claudia saw they had made up their minds, she resigned herself to Agnes's peculiar choice and would not be left out of the decorating. They went back to the house for the apples, popcorn garlands, and strings of cranberries and nuts, which they wrapped around the Frazier fir by tossing one end of the strings into the highest branches they could reach and unwinding as they walked around the tree. With bits of twine, they tied apples by their stems to the ends of branches, which dipped slightly beneath the weight. Inspired, Sylvia sent Agnes back to the house for cookie cutters, which they used to carve stars and circles from packed snow, frosted shapes they arranged on the boughs like ornaments. Claudia turned out to be quite good at it. Soon she was enjoying herself as much as the others, and she led them in Christmas carols, including a few of her own invention.

"Don't sit under the Christmas tree, with anyone else but me," Claudia sang, and the others burst into laughter. She pretended to be insulted. "Don't laugh. I'm composing a holiday classic."

"I'm sure Glenn Miller can't wait to record it," said Sylvia.

Afterward, they stood back to admire their work. Agnes glowed with happiness, and Claudia admitted that their tree was pretty in its own way. "It's certainly unique," Sylvia agreed, and the women linked arms as they trudged through the snow back to the manor, pulling the toboggan behind them.

The next morning, Sylvia's father felt well enough to accompany the women to church. The mood of the congregation was more subdued than celebratory, more longing than joyful. Sylvia knew that nearly every person gathered there yearned for a brother, father, husband, or son overseas, or was grieving for someone lost to the war. Even the pastor had a brother serving in France, and in his sermon he referred to the men they all missed and their longing for peace.

"We must not give in to despair," the pastor said. "We must have faith that the

Lord who loves us will not abandon us. Though far too many of us have sewn gold stars on the service banners displayed in our front windows, though so many of us mourn, we must not believe that God has ceased loving us. He has not forgotten us. In our moments of weakness, we may fear that we walk alone, but we must never forget that God has sent us the light of his love and mercy. The light shines in the darkness, and the darkness shall not overcome it.

"The miracle of Christmas is that in sending to us His only Son, whose birth we celebrate this morning, God kindled a light in the darkness that shrouded the earth, a light that continues to shine brightly and will never be extinguished. Today, my dear brothers and sisters, we are confronted by darkness — the darkness of war, of tyranny, of oppression, of loneliness, of evil manifest in the world. Today, with the entire world at war, this darkness seems very deep indeed, but we must not forget that Jesus Christ brought the light of peace, and hope, and reconciliation into the world, and no darkness shall ever quench it. Each of us must bring light into the world, so that the darkness will not prevail."

Transfixed by his compassionate words, heart aching for her husband, Sylvia found herself fighting back tears of grief and anguish. If James and Richard did not return to her, she did not know how she could endure it. She knew that she could not. She was desperate for the light the pastor had spoken of to shine through the darkness of her life, but she was so afraid, and so lonely. The darkness surrounding her was so opaque she feared no illumination could penetrate it. In silence, she cried out for God's mercy, for the comfort only He could provide.

A hand clasped hers — Claudia's — and she reached out her other hand to Agnes, and then Sylvia understood. They were all lonely and afraid. They had to be light for one another.

The three Bergstrom sisters held fast to one another for the rest of the service. They held hands still as they rose to sing the final hymn. As the last notes of the song faded away, Sylvia felt peace settling into her heart, and she whispered a prayer of thanks for her two sisters. They would sustain one another, whatever came, whatever darkness threatened them.

Back at home, the family breakfasted on the famous Bergstrom apple strudel and coffee, and then gathered in the ballroom to exchange gifts. Sylvia's eyes filled with tears when she unwrapped Agnes's gift — a beautifully knitted cap, receiving blanket, and booties done in a seed stitch in the softest, finest of blue-and-pink stripes.

"Where did you ever find the yarn for this?" asked Sylvia, fingering the precious garments.

"I found a worn layette in the attic," confessed Agnes. "Moths had eaten through the blanket, but I washed it thoroughly and most of the yarn was still useable. I wish I could say it was new."

"Nonsense," declared Sylvia. "It's as good as new. Better. It has family history."

Agnes was so pleased she blushed.

Later, after the presents were opened and admired, the women read aloud from their men's letters, saved for this occasion so that they would feel as if the family had reunited on Christmas Day. It had taken all of Sylvia's willpower not to tear open James's letter as soon as it had arrived a week before, but now she was grateful she had agreed to Claudia's proposal. The men had been promised a hot Christmas dinner instead of the usual rations, James had written. Turkey with dressing, cranberry sauce, mashed potatoes, green beans, and apple pie for dessert. It wouldn't compare to anything Gerda Bergstrom might have prepared, but to the men hungry for a taste of home, it would seem like a feast for a king.

Harold reported a mild case of dysentery; Richard was learning how to drive a tank. Andrew had sent one letter to them all, thanking them for the pictures of the girls on the back steps of the manor. "I don't have a sweetheart to write home to," he confessed, "so I especially welcome your letters." He promised to look after Richard and thanked Sylvia's father for the memories of the best Christmas he had ever spent, which, he said, would be a comfort to him this season spent in the heat of the South Pacific, far from the snowy forests and fields of home.

Sylvia's father cleared his throat several times as the last letter was read, and when Agnes finished reading, he went alone to the window and gazed outside to the gray sky that spoke of snow to come. Sylvia wished there had been more letters. Cousin Elizabeth had not written for the third or possibly fourth Christmas in a row; Sylvia had lost track. But she knew that what her father longed for most he could not have: for his son to walk in the door that moment, his wife to be standing at his side holding his hand, his brother to be making jokes and teasing the children, his great-aunt Lucinda and his mother to be holding court in their chairs by the hearth.

"Sylvia," he said suddenly, beckoning to her. "Come take a look at this."

She went to him and looked out the window. Just beyond the elms on the other side of the creek, she saw Agnes's Christmas tree, simply but beautifully adorned. As she watched, she detected movement, and suddenly a doe and fawn emerged from the woods and carefully picked their way through the crust that had formed on top of the snow. They approached the Christmas tree, and the doe stretched out her head to nibble a popcorn garland. Her fawn cautiously bit into an apple.

Sylvia's smile broadened as a flurry of motion heralded the arrival of a flock of chickadees. Soon other birds joined in the feast, and squirrels as well, busily harvesting the popcorn, fruits, and nuts from the Christmas tree.

Claudia and Agnes came to see what engrossed them. "Our tree," Claudia lamented when she understood what was happening, but Agnes laughed out loud.

"I knew that nest wasn't abandoned," she cried. "I knew that tree was still a home to someone."

"If it wasn't before, it is now," remarked Sylvia, and her father chuckled.

"We should make this a new tradition," said Agnes as they watched the feast. "Every year we should bring in one tree for ourselves and decorate that one for the animals."

Amused, Sylvia asked, "What if next Christmas Richard wants to cut down that tree and bring it indoors?"

"I'll talk him out of it," said Agnes, without a moment's hesitation.

"Next year we will all be together again," said Claudia, with such resolve that for a moment they all shared her certainty that it would be so. "Next Christmas, the war will be over and the boys will be home."

And Claudia and Harold might be the newlyweds, Sylvia thought. It would be their turn to bring in the tree. Their nephew or niece would be enjoying his or her first Christmas, and God willing, in the years to come many cousins would join her, filling the house with love and laughter again.

Let this be our Christmas miracle, Sylvia prayed, watching from the window as the wildlife of Elm Creek Manor enjoyed an unexpected Christmas feast while snow began to fall.

Chapter Five

The blessings of Christmas lingered in Sylvia's heart into the New Year, sustaining her through the difficult last months of the war.

But the Christmas future with her husband and child that she had prayed for did not come to pass. Of the four men they were longing to see that day, only Andrew and Harold returned.

A few months after Christmas, James died attempting to save Richard's life, determined to the end to protect him as he had promised.

The shock of the news sent Sylvia into premature labor. Her daughter, born too soon, fought for life for three days, but eventually slipped away.

Devastated, maddened by grief, Sylvia remembered little of the aftermath. As if looking through a fog of sorrow, she saw herself lying in a hospital bed, holding her baby's small, still body and weeping. She recalled begging the doctors to release her so she might attend the funeral of her father, who had collapsed from stroke, unable to bear the shock of so much loss.

Eventually Sylvia was released from the hospital and sent home. For weeks afterward, she felt as if the world were shrouded in a thick woolen batting. Sounds were less distinct. Colors were duller. Everything seemed to move more slowly.

Gradually the numbness that pervaded her began to recede, replaced by the most unbearable pain. Her beloved James was gone, and she still did not know how he had died. Her daughter was gone. She would never hold her again. Her darling little brother was gone. Her father was gone. The litany repeated itself relentlessly in her mind until she believed she would go mad.

A few hesitant visitors from the Waterford Quilting Guild came by to express their sympathies and see what, if anything, they might do to help, but Sylvia refused to see them. Eventually they stopped coming.

The war ended. Harold returned to Elm Creek Manor thinner, more anxious — a pale shadow of the man who had left. Perhaps seeking a distraction or a return to normalcy, Claudia threw herself into planning her wedding. As her matron of honor, Sylvia was expected to help, but though she tried, she could not summon up any interest and had difficulty remembering the details of the tasks Claudia assigned to her.

One day a few weeks before the wedding, Andrew paid an unexpected visit on his way from Philadelphia to a new job in Detroit. Sylvia was glad to see him. He walked with a new limp and sat stiffly in his chair as if still in the service, and although he was pleasant to everyone else, he had barely a cold word for Harold, who seemed to go out of his way to avoid Andrew. Sylvia found this odd, since she had always heard that veterans shared a bond almost like that of brothers. Perhaps seeing each other dredged up memories of the war that were still too painful to bear.

That evening after dinner, Andrew found Sylvia alone in the library. He took her hand and pulled her over to the sofa, shaking from the effort to suppress his anger and grief. He had seen everything from a bluff overlooking the beach where they had been killed. He had been a witness to it all and powerless to help. He offered to tell her how her brother and husband died, but warned her she would find no comfort in the truth.

Without thinking of the consequences, Sylvia told him to tell her what he had seen. Haltingly, every word paining him, he described how Richard had come under friendly fire, how James had raced to his rescue, how he would have succeeded with the help of one more man. How Harold had hidden himself rather than risk his own life. How Andrew had run straight down the bluff to the beach where his friends lay dying, knowing that he would never make it in time.

"I'm so sorry, Sylvia," said Andrew, his voice breaking. "He saved me when we were kids, but I couldn't save him. I'm so sorry."

Sylvia held him as he wept, but she had no words to comfort him.

Andrew left Elm Creek Manor the next morning. Sylvia brooded in silent rage as the days passed and the plans for the wedding continued. Finally, she could keep silent no longer. Her sister had to know the truth about the man she intended to marry.

But to Sylvia's shock and outrage, Claudia denied the truth, blaming Sylvia's accusations on jealousy that Harold had come back and James had not. Torn apart by this unexpected betrayal, Sylvia left Elm Creek Manor that day, unable to bear the sight of the man who had allowed her husband and brother to die, unable to live with a sister who preferred a disloyal lie to the truth. Into two suitcases she packed all she could carry — photographs, letters from Richard and James, the sewing basket she had received for Christmas the year before her mother died. Everything else she left behind — beloved childhood treasures, favorite books, unfinished projects, the Christmas Quilt. Everything except memories and grief.

She intended never to return.

Fifty years later, when she received word of Claudia's death, she tried to find someone else to inherit the manor — a distant relation she had never met, anyone. She even hired a private detective, but his search promptly turned up nothing — so promptly that she sometimes suspected he had not searched as thoroughly as his fees merited. But with no one to pass on the burden to, she returned to Elm Creek Manor as the sole heir to the Bergstrom estate.

And here she would live out her days, no longer consumed by regrets, thanks to the intercession of Sarah and Matt McClure.

She would always long for what might have been, but she would also accept with gratitude the blessings that had come to her late in life.

If only Claudia were there to share them with her.

She heard the back door open and Sarah and Matt came in, laughing. "We found a tree," Matt called.

Sylvia rose to join them.

In the back entry, a six-foot blue spruce lay on the floor. "What do you think?" Sarah asked, as she and Matt removed their coats and boots.

"It doesn't look like much, lying down," Sylvia remarked. She glanced at her watch. Bringing in the tree had taken them a respectable hour and a half. That spoke well for the couple — better, in fact, than she had expected. They had clearly not wasted time in argument, nor in indecisiveness, with neither willing to hold to a position for fear of offending the other. Nor had they returned too quickly, indicating that only one of them had chosen the tree and the other had been unwilling to suggest an alternative, or had spoken up only to be ignored. If a husband and wife could not work together in a simple task like choosing a Christmas tree, it did not bode well for the more important decisions they would face in their life together.

Sylvia thought Sarah and Matt would do just fine.

"Shall we set it up in the west sitting room?" asked Sarah.

"All in good time," said Sylvia. "First I need to pay a call on someone I've too long neglected, and I would appreciate a lift."

Sylvia sat on the passenger side of Sarah and Matt's red pickup truck, the pinecone wreath she and her mother had made on her lap. They passed the old red barn Hans Bergstrom had built into the hillside, rounded a curve, and drove downhill along the edge of the orchard. The gravel road narrowed as they entered the woods, bouncing and jolting over the potholes, until they emerged a quarter of a mile later and turned left onto the paved county highway that led to the town of Waterford proper.

"Do you mind telling me where we're going?" asked Sarah. "Or is it a surprise?"

Sylvia gestured toward the road ahead. "Just keep heading into town."

Sarah shrugged and did as she was told.

As they drove north, the rural landscape

gave way to planned neighborhoods that had sprung up on the farmland during Sylvia's absence, and a couple of strip malls that looked like every other strip mall one might find in the more urban regions of Pennsylvania. As they approached the heart of town, the buildings showed more age, and more character, though most of the shops Sylvia had frequented as a young woman had been replaced by quirky boutiques, restaurants, and bars catering to the students and faculty of Waterford College.

"Turn here," Sylvia said as they approached Church Street.

A block from the town square, Sylvia asked Sarah to park in the church's lot. As Sylvia gazed through the windshield at the small churchyard enclosed within a low iron fence, Sarah asked, "Do you want me to come with you?"

Sylvia roused herself and unbuckled her seatbelt. "No, dear," she said. "I need a word in private."

Carrying the wreath, she made her way carefully across the parking lot and passed through the gate into the cemetery. Like the parking lot, the walking paths had been cleared of the previous night's snowfall, but a light dusting of snow had blown across the paths since then, and in the footprints left behind Sylvia read the longings of the other mourners who had come to pay respects that day. Few had been buried in that churchyard since the 1950s after the larger cemetery was established east of town, but the Bergstroms owned a family plot, and many generations had been laid to rest in the shadow of the old church steeple.

The lilac bush her father had planted remained, dormant now in the depths of winter but thriving, larger than she remembered. In the spring, the winds would shower her parents' graves with fragrant blossoms. Sylvia gazed down upon the headstone engraved with both of their names, the dates they had died fifteen years apart. They had made the most of the time granted to them, and Sylvia wished she had followed their example. She understood too late how wise they had been.

She said a silent prayer and looked about for the headstone she had seen only once, a few days after her return to Waterford. It was smaller than her parents', low to the ground and engraved only with Claudia's married name, date of birth, and the day she had died. It was simple and modest, chosen by two women from the church, who apologized when they showed it to Sylvia. Claudia had set aside a little money for her burial, they said, but it did not stretch far. If they had known she had surviving family, they would have waited, but as it was they followed Claudia's instructions the best they could. If Sylvia liked, she could replace the headstone with something more suitable.

"No," Sylvia had told them. "This is what she requested, and it will do. Thank you for seeing to it for me."

As she had on that first visit two years before, Sylvia studied the headstone and wondered why Claudia had selected this plot for herself and had buried Harold in the newer, larger cemetery. Why had she not wanted to be interred beside her husband, as their parents had done? Why was Harold's headstone as stark as Claudia's, with no fond epitaph to show the world that he had once been loved?

Sylvia suspected she knew. If Claudia had come to believe the truth about Harold's role in Richard's and James's deaths, Sylvia could not imagine how she had endured living so many years as his wife. Elm Creek Manor was not so large that they could have avoided each other indefinitely. Sylvia knew so little of Claudia's life after her abrupt departure. Agnes had remained at Elm Creek Manor for several years until she left to marry a history professor from Waterford College, but she had told Sylvia very little of those days, probably wishing to spare her pain. Sylvia had so few clues to tell her of the woman her sister had become — a few unfinished quilts, the overgrown gardens, the dilapidated state of the manor — but none of her own words, not one single photograph. Forever Claudia would remain fixed in Sylvia's memory precisely as she was the day their final argument compelled Sylvia from their home.

If only Sylvia had remembered how they had been each other's light in the darkness on the last Christmas of the war. If only she had remembered that, and come home.

"I'm sorry," Sylvia said aloud. "I'm sorry I was too proud to come home. I'm sorry I never had the chance to apologize to you. All these years I've blamed you for driving me away, but that's not why I left, not really. It's not because you married Harold. It's not even because I couldn't bear the sight of him, although it did take me a long time to stop hating him."

Sylvia inhaled deeply, her nostrils stinging from the cold, her breath emerging as a stream of ghostly mist. "I ran away because I was afraid. I didn't think I could endure the daily reminders of the happiness I once had and had lost. Now I know I should have stayed. Together you and I and Agnes could have helped one another bear our burdens. Instead I ran away, but I took my grief with me, and I've regretted it ever since."

She bent down to lay the wreath on Claudia's grave, arranging the red velvet ribbon with care. Then she straightened. "I wish —" She hesitated. "I wish I knew that wherever you are, you've forgiven me."

She murmured a quiet prayer, then turned and made her way back to the waiting truck. Sarah offered her a sympathetic smile as she took her seat, but thankfully did not trouble her with questions.

Back at the manor, Sylvia and Sarah found the Christmas tree still lying on the floor just inside the back entrance. Matt was in the west sitting room, putting the last screws into a metal tree stand he must have purchased earlier that day because Sylvia had never seen it before. He had moved furniture aside to clear a corner of the room for the tree, setting the sewing machine against the wall and stacking the pieces of the Christmas Quilt neatly on the sofa. Boxes of ornaments lay scattered on the floor between the coffee table and the two armchairs by the window.

Matt looked up and smiled as they entered. "Just in time," he said. "Sarah, could you give me a hand with the tree?"

Sylvia scooted out of the way while the young people hefted the tree and carried it from the hallway into the sitting room. She offered directions as they wrestled it into the tree stand, pushing it this way and that until it stood straight and tall. Then they set it back into the corner, rotating the stand so that its best side faced out.

It was a beautiful tree, full and tall and fragrant.

Sylvia nodded her approval as Sarah and Matt stepped back for a better look. "You chose well," she praised them. "I believe you must have found the finest tree in the forest."

"There was another one we liked better, closer to the manor between the creek and the barn," said Sarah. "We decided not to cut it down because there was a bird's nest in it."

Sylvia gave her a long look. "Indeed?"

"The nest looked abandoned to me," said Matt, "but we decided not to disturb it just in case."

"I understand completely," said Sylvia, inspecting the tree. "I see you had to trim off a bit here," she said, indicating the top of the tree, where the severed trunk was hidden among the boughs. "Was it crooked, or did you think the tree would be too tall?"

"We didn't cut off the top," said Matt. "See how the wood has weathered? The top of this tree was cut off long ago. We just took off the next six feet down."

Sylvia stared at him, then at Sarah. "What you mean is that when you had that arborist out here last spring, he pruned this tree."

Matt shook his head. "No, that's not what I meant. When I say long ago, I mean decades. Maybe between forty and sixty years, but I'm just guessing."

"Fifty-five," murmured Sylvia. It was an unlikely coincidence. Out of all the trees in the forest, Sarah and Matt had just happened to pick the same blue spruce that she and James had chosen? She was too skeptical a soul to believe that.

But how could they have known?

She shook off a quickening of excitement. Coincidence, she told herself firmly. Nothing more.

They strung tiny white lights upon the

tree, the candles of Sylvia's childhood gone the way of other hazards they had once accepted with blissful ignorance. As Sarah's CD player serenaded them with carols, they adorned the tree with the beloved, familiar ornaments from Sylvia's youth — the ceramic figurines from Germany, the sparkling crystal teardrops from New York City, carved wooden angels with woolen hair from Italy. Beneath the tree, Sarah arranged the nativity scene Sylvia's grandfather had carved, while Matt placed Richard's soldier nutcracker and Grandmother's green sleigh music box on the table. Sylvia found the paper angels she and Claudia had made in Sunday school, yellowed and curled with age, but so dear to her that she would not dream of leaving them out. She placed them in prominent places high upon the tree, Claudia's on one branch and her own on the opposite side of the tree exactly even with her sister's — not one branch higher, not one lower.

"What should we put on the top of the tree?" asked Sarah, digging through the boxes. "I haven't found an obvious tree topper, like a star or an angel or something."

"For many years, we left the highest bough bare," said Sylvia.

"Why? Is that symbolic of something?"

Loss, Sylvia almost said. "No. For many years we used a red-and-gold glass star, but it went missing one year and we never replaced it."

"I think I know why," said Matt, nodding toward the paper angels with a grin. "You and your sister fought over whose angel should be above the other's. Neither of you would give in, so you didn't use anything."

"You know us too well," said Sylvia lightly, although until that moment, it had never occurred to her to wonder why no one had ever suggested using their angels in that fashion. Perhaps the bare top of the tree was meant to prick the prankster's conscience, an annual reminder that the loss of the star had not been forgotten. More likely, their father had not wanted to suggest anything that might stir up an argument between the sisters.

Just then, Sylvia heard a knock on the back door and a slight pause before it swung open. "Hello," a voice called out. "Is anyone home? Don't bother denying it because we saw the truck in the lot."

Sylvia smiled, recognizing the voice. "We're in here, Agnes."

A moment later, Agnes appeared in the

doorway, petite and white-haired, her blue eyes beaming behind pink-tinted glasses. Behind her stood her eldest daughter, Cassandra, a head taller than her mother but with the same blue eyes and raven black hair of her youth, bearing only the first traces of gray. They had both removed their coats, and Cassandra carried a white bakery box.

"Merry Christmas," Agnes greeted them. She embraced Sylvia first, then Sarah and Matt. "What a beautiful tree."

"Sarah and Matt chose it," Sylvia said.

"Naturally. They are the newlyweds." Agnes's merriment turned to surprise as she spotted the Christmas Quilt on the sofa behind Sylvia. "My goodness. You've brought out the Christmas Quilt. You're putting it together at last."

"Yes, well — Sarah is," said Sylvia.

Agnes hurried over and picked up a section of the quilt where Sarah had joined Feathered Stars and holly plumes together. "It's just as lovely as I remembered. Your mother's appliqué was my inspiration, you know. I never forgot her beautiful handiwork. When Joe asked me to marry him, I was determined to learn to appliqué so I could make us a beautiful heirloom wedding quilt."

"I never knew that," said Sylvia.

"You should see it," said Cassandra, smiling at her mother. "It's exquisite. All those beautiful rosebuds."

"I wouldn't say exquisite," said Agnes, but they could all tell she was pleased. "Not with so many mistakes. I was just a beginner, in over my head."

"We all have to start somewhere," said Sarah.

"I couldn't agree more." Agnes gave the holly plumes a fond caress and returned them gently to the sofa. "I'm so pleased to see someone working on this quilt after so many years."

"I'm surprised Claudia didn't throw it out after I left," said Sylvia. "She already associated it with so many unpleasant memories even before I took it up, and I'm sure my departure didn't help. I suppose she was all too willing to pack it away where she would never have to lay eyes on it again."

Agnes peered at her curiously, her pink lenses giving her a rosy, girlish air. "Why, no, that's not the case at all. Claudia worked on it every Christmas that I lived here. She brought it out on St. Nicholas Day and put it away with the rest of the Christmas things on the Feast of the Three

Kings. For the few years that I lived here, Claudia fully intended to finish that quilt. Even when times grew difficult between her and Harold, she had her heart set on it."

"But —" Sylvia glanced at the sofa and swiftly counted five Variable Star blocks. "I know she finished those Variable Stars long before I left home."

"I didn't say she made more Variable Stars," said Agnes. "You really didn't notice? How many Log Cabin blocks did you make, Sylvia? Fifteen or twenty?"

"That sounds about right," said Sylvia.

"There are far more than that here," said Sarah. "I counted at least fifty."

"That can't be." Sylvia counted for herself, examining the quality of the needlework as she did. Each of fifty-two blocks was as finely sewn and precise as any block Sylvia had ever made. She could not distinguish between her work and her sister's. "But why would she make more of the pattern I selected rather than her own?"

"Maybe she understood why you chose as you did," said Sarah. "Apparently she trusted your judgment more than you thought. Maybe this was her way of telling you so."

Perhaps it was true. Could it be that all

those Christmases Sylvia had spent alone, longing for home, Claudia had been missing her, too?

For Sylvia it was all too overwhelming. She sat down on her favorite chair by the window and stared at the quilt, still in pieces, but coming together thanks to Sarah's loving attention.

"I was afraid, since the Christmas decorations had been stored away so long," she said softly, "that Claudia stopped celebrating Christmas after I left."

"You forgot about the aluminum tree," said Sarah. "Remember? Maybe she couldn't have a traditional Bergstrom holiday on her own, but she did celebrate Christmas."

"And of course there was also the — Oh, my goodness. You're not the only forgetful one." Agnes beckoned her daughter forward. "Cassie, would you give Sylvia her present, please?"

Cassandra placed the white cardboard bakery box on Sylvia's lap. "You should open it now," she said, smiling. "Don't wait for Christmas morning."

Sylvia lifted the lid, and on any other day she would have been astonished to find an exact replica of the famous Bergstrom strudel, but not that day.

"Where on earth did you buy this?" she exclaimed. "I thought the German bakery on College Avenue closed years ago."

"She didn't buy it," said Cassandra proudly. "She made it. And what a production it was!"

"Claudia taught you," said Sylvia in wonder. "She did keep the old traditions."

"Not this one, I'm afraid," said Agnes. "We made strudel the Christmas after you left, but it was such a bleak and empty season without you, without Richard and James, that we couldn't even bear to eat it. We made two and gave them both away. As far as I know, that was the last time anyone made strudel in the Bergstrom kitchen."

"And you remembered the recipe yourself after all those years." When Agnes shook her head, Sylvia said, "Then Claudia wrote it down for you."

"No, in fact, many years after I married, I came by and asked Claudia for it, but she said it had never been written down, and that she had forgotten it. Then, years later, she sent me a Christmas card with the recipe enclosed. She remembered how I had asked for it, and so she got it from a distant relation out west. A second cousin, I believe."

Sylvia could scarcely breathe. "Do you

remember her name? When was it she wrote to Claudia?"

Agnes shook her head. "I'm afraid I don't recall."

Sylvia's heart sank. It was, she knew, too much to hope for.

"But I have the letter at home."

In the twenty minutes it took Cassandra to return to her mother's home for the letter, Sylvia's thoughts raced with possibilities. The only relative she knew of who had gone to live "out west" was Elizabeth, and although Sylvia had always called her cousin, as the daughter of Sylvia's great-uncle George, it would have been more accurate to call her a second cousin.

"Oh, what could be keeping Cassandra?" exclaimed Sylvia, pacing in the sitting room.

"It's ten minutes there and ten minutes back," said Agnes soothingly. "She'll be here soon."

"But what if she can't find it?"

Agnes assured her this was unlikely. "Just bring the whole box," she had instructed her daughter, referring to a small cedar chest in which she kept some of Richard's belongings. She had described its location, inside a larger steamer trunk in the back of Agnes's bedroom closet. It ought to be easy to find.

After what seemed to Sylvia an interminable wait, Cassandra returned, the small wooden box in her hands. "I would have been back sooner," she said breathlessly as she gave the box to her mother and pulled off her coat and gloves, "but I had trouble staying on the road in your woods."

"We must do something about that road," said Sylvia. "Well, Agnes? Is it there?"

"It was there this morning when I used the recipe," she said, with a hint of amusement. "Would you please sit down? You're rattling the Christmas ornaments with all of that pacing."

Sylvia dropped into her favorite chair and clasped her hands anxiously while Agnes took a seat in the nearest armchair. Sylvia held her breath as Agnes lifted the lid and removed a folded sheet of yellowed, unlined paper. With a fond smile, she passed it to Sylvia.

Sylvia slipped on her glasses, unfolded the page, and read:

December 6, 1964

Dear Claudia,

How wonderful it was to hear from you after so many years! Your letter was truly the best Christmas gift I am likely to receive. I apologize for not writing to you for so long. I suppose I fell out of habit. (Isn't that a dreadful thing to say about keeping in touch with one's family? That it should be a habit, like getting your daily exercise and remembering to take your vitamins.)

All excuses aside, I promise to send you a longer letter soon, full of news of me and the family. For now, I assure you that we're doing all right out here in sunny Southern California. It's more crowded than it used to be, but the weather is fine and we like it. I'll add you to my Christmas letter list, so check your mailbox in a week or two for more news than you probably can stand about us.

While we're on the subject, would it have hurt you to send some news about yourself and the rest of the family at Elm Creek Manor? How are you? How's Harold? How is my dear little Sylvia and baby brother Richard? I suppose they aren't so little anymore. Please tell Sylvia to write to me and tell her I'm sorry her old cousin hasn't written in so long. It would serve me right if she's forgotten me entirely.

Well, on to the purpose of this letter. I still make the famous Bergstrom strudel every Christmas, winning praise from all who are privileged enough to taste it. I still bake it in the old way, measuring by touch and sight and taste rather than cups and teaspoons. But since you are my sweet little cousin (and perhaps because I have a guilty conscience for neglecting you so long), I made strudel this morning, first measuring my ingredients the old way, and then scooping each one into measuring cups so I could give you the standard measurements you asked for. You'll find the recipe on the back of this page. If my measurements are off a pinch of this or that, please accept my apologies. It probably won't matter. Once you start making the strudel again, I'm sure it will all come back to you.

An early Merry Christmas to you and the family. Please send me a letter packed full of news next time. I know you are capable of it! And make it soon, please. I miss you throughout the year, but especially at Christmas.

With Much Love from Your Cousin,
Elizabeth

Sylvia turned over the letter and found a recipe printed in Elizabeth's neat hand on the back, just as she had promised.

She read the date again. Elizabeth was still in Southern California in 1964, and — Sylvia checked the letter to be sure — she had a family. Elizabeth would be ninety-three if she were still alive, but even if she were not, perhaps her descendants were, regardless of what that private detective had concluded.

"Do you have a return address?" she asked, her voice choked with emotion.

"I'm sorry." Agnes shook her head, sympathetic. "Claudia sent me only that page. I don't know what became of the envelope."

"I understand." Still, it was something to go on, and perhaps that Christmas letter Elizabeth had promised Claudia was somewhere in the manor. Sylvia had not gone through all of Claudia's papers; there were so many. She had every reason to hope an address could be found among them.

"Why don't you show her the rest, Mom?" prompted Cassandra. "The letters and things?"

Agnes went pink. "Oh, not the letters. Not even after all this time. Forgive me, Sylvia, but Richard was a romantic and I couldn't bear for anyone to see them. I don't even know if Joe suspected I had kept this box of things hidden away from him. He wasn't the jealous sort, but even so . . ."

"I won't pry into your romance with my baby brother," said Sylvia, amused. She tried to peer into the box, but the lid blocked her view. "If you have anything in that box of a less private nature, I would be grateful if you would share it with me."

"Certainly." Agnes looked much relieved. "Some of these things you've seen before, but it was so long ago . . ."

She handed over a stack of photographs: Richard and Andrew at school, Richard and Agnes on the front steps of Independence Hall, the three friends laughing on a sunny day along the Delaware River with the Philadelphia skyline behind them. There were other snapshots of Richard alone, including a formal portrait in uniform and other snapshots taken during the war. Sylvia lingered over a photograph of Richard and James in fatigues, arms slung over each other's shoulders, grinning.

"You should keep that one," said Agnes.

Sylvia thanked her softly.

"I suppose you should keep this, too," Agnes remarked, taking from the box a ruby-and-gold glass star, with eight serrated points resembling the Feathered Star blocks Great-Aunt Lucinda had made so long ago. Only a small chip in one of the golden tips and a hairline seam where a ruby star point had been broken off and reattached with glue distinguished it from the one in Sylvia's memory.

Sylvia stared, shocked into silence. "Where on earth did you find *that?*" she finally managed.

"It was Richard's." Agnes turned the star over in her hands, shook her head in bemusement, and handed it to Sylvia. "I'm not quite sure what the story behind it is. It was December, right before the semester holiday, when I first saw it. We were all out together one day when Andrew suddenly pulled this from his overcoat pocket, repaired exactly as you see it here, gave it to Richard, and said, 'Merry Christmas. I guess you'll win the prize this year.' Richard laughed like it was the funniest joke he had ever heard and said, 'I knew it was you! I knew it all along. I'm never playing poker with you again.' And then they both had a good laugh, and Richard said, 'I can't wait to see their faces when they wake up Christmas morning and find this on the tree.' But he must have forgotten about it in all the commotion because he didn't put it on the tree after all."

"What commotion?" asked Sarah.

Agnes threw Sylvia an embarrassed glance. "Well, in a manner of speaking, I invited myself along when Richard went home from school for the holidays. I met him at the train station with my suitcase and asked if I could join him. He said yes without a moment's hesitation, although I'm sure he knew my parents didn't know of my plans."

"I suspected as much," declared Sylvia. "I knew there must have been a very good reason Richard had not warned me you were coming."

"Warned?" echoed Cassandra.

"Told," Sylvia hastily amended.

"The star was among Richard's belongings from school," Agnes explained. "He packed up so quickly after enlisting that I never took the time to sort through his trunk. After he died — well, it was simply too painful. I opened the trunk to put this box and his uniform and a few other things inside, but I couldn't bear to sort through everything. When I left to marry Joe, I took the trunk with me. A few years later I wanted to see these old photos again, and that's when I stumbled across the star."

"But why didn't you tell us you had found it?" asked Sylvia.

Agnes shrugged. "I didn't know it was missing."

"It isn't missing anymore," said Sarah. "Sylvia, why don't you do the honors?"

Holding the star tenderly, Sylvia rose, went to the Christmas tree, and reached up to the highest bough, where she carefully fixed the ruby-and-gold glass star to the cut tree trunk. It caught the sunlight streaming in through the west windows and sent reflections of red and gold dancing on the walls and ceiling and floor just as it had on the long ago Christmas when Elizabeth had hidden the star beneath her pillow and her father had lifted her up in his strong arms to adorn the tree Uncle William and Aunt Nellie had chosen. From a distance the repair and the chip were hardly noticeable.

She would not go so far as to call any one of the unusual incidents of that day a Christmas miracle. The standard for miracle, she thought, stood a bit higher. But taken as a whole — that business with the tree, hearing from Elizabeth, even in an old letter — well, she would be a fool to ignore the signs. She didn't need a burning bush or Jacob Marley rattling chains in the halls to know when she ought to pay attention.

Very well, Claudia, she thought, smiling. *I can take a hint.*

Sylvia was forgiven. She knew that now. Despite their differences, despite Sylvia's mistakes, her sister loved her, and always had. But the realization was bittersweet because Claudia was not there to enjoy the wonder of that Christmas Eve, the Christmas that joy and hope returned to Elm Creek Manor.

But she could still make a difference in the life of a friend.

Sylvia turned to Sarah. "I've tried reasoning with you. I've hinted and suggested and resorted to subterfuge, but nothing has worked. But you must do it, and I won't take no for an answer."

Sarah stared at her. "No for an answer to what?"

"Visiting your mother for Christmas."

Sarah rolled her eyes. "We've been over this. I thought you understood —"

"I understand, all right. I understand that you and your mother need to make peace before you end up like me — realizing too late where I went wrong and reconciling with memories instead of living, breathing people." She tapped Sarah on the chest, and the young woman was too startled to step back out of the way. "You, young lady, are not going to make that mistake. I'm going to see to it."

Warily, Sarah asked, "What exactly did you have in mind?"

"I'm throwing you out."

"What?"

"Just for the holiday. You're welcome back any time after Christmas."

Sarah shook her head. "This is crazy."

"It's been a crazy sort of day. I suppose it's infectious." Sylvia held up her hands to forestall an argument. "Now, I've made up my mind, so don't argue. I realize I can't force you to visit your mother. I suppose you could sleep outside in the truck or take a hotel room somewhere, but I can only hope you won't be that stubborn."

"Sylvia . . ." Sarah studied her, shaking her head in bewilderment. "Why is this so important to you?"

Sylvia grasped her gently by the shoulders. "Because you are important to me. I don't want you to look back on your life someday and wonder if you did everything you could to make the best possible use of your time on this earth. We all are responsible for bringing the peace of Christmas into the world, Sarah. Starting with our own families."

"I can't make peace with my mother if she doesn't meet me halfway," Sarah retorted, but then she hesitated. "If it means that much to you, I'll try. I'll go see her. But I can't promise that she'll welcome us with open arms."

"As long as you greet her with an open mind, that's all I ask."

"What about you?" asked Sarah. "You can't spend Christmas here alone."

Sylvia shrugged. "We'll have our celebration tonight. You and Matthew can leave for your mother's place first thing in the morning."

"Sounds good to me," offered Matt.

Sarah was not satisfied. "That still leaves you alone on Christmas Day."

"Sylvia can spend Christmas at my home," said Agnes. "With me and the girls and the grandkids. There's always room for one more."

"No, there isn't," said Sylvia, remembering their phone conversation earlier that day. "So you and your family should spend Christmas with me."

Agnes brightened. "Here at Elm Creek Manor?"

"We could spend it in the barn if you prefer but the manor will be warmer." Sylvia smiled. "Why not here? We have a tree, all the fixings for a Christmas dinner, and plenty of room for the children to run around."

Agnes looked inquiringly at her daughter, who said, "It's fine with me, Mom, and I know Louisa will agree. She was worried about the kids trashing your house, so this will be a load off her mind."

"The children are more than welcome to trash my house instead," declared Sylvia.

Agnes beamed, and for a moment, Sylvia glimpsed in her lined face the girl her brother had loved. "In that case, we'd be delighted to accept your invitation."

On Christmas morning, Sylvia, Sarah, and Matt rose early for church and returned home to a breakfast of Agnes's apple strudel. The famous Bergstrom recipe was as delicious as Sylvia remembered. The cinnamon spiced apples and flaky crust immediately took Sylvia back to those Christmas mornings of childhood, when the people she loved gathered around the table and reminisced about Christmases past and absent loved ones. Gerda Bergstrom could not have done any better.

They exchanged gifts, and after Sylvia reassured them that she would be perfectly content, Sarah and Matt loaded their suitcases into the red pickup and drove off to Uniontown to spend a few days with Sarah's mother. Sarah called later that afternoon to tell Sylvia that her mother had loved the Hunter's Star quilt. Carol had given Sarah and Matt jeans, identical blue-and-white striped sweaters, and knit Penn State hats. "Can you believe it?" said Sarah in a low voice so she would not be overheard. "Matching outfits, like we were five-year-old twins or something." But she sounded pleased.

Not long after Sarah and Matt departed, Agnes and her brood showed up, and the children promptly filled the manor with enough noise and play and laughter for twice their number. Santa had apparently gone on a Christmas Eve shopping spree, too — in a red pickup rather than a sleigh — because there were toys for each child beneath the tree. After some consideration, Sylvia decided against reviving the tradition of hiding the ruby-and-gold glass star.

It was a wonderful, blessed day.

When her guests departed, Sylvia tidied the kitchen and settled down in the sitting room with a cup of tea, her heart content. She put on her glasses and read Elizabeth's letter once more, then sighed, folded it, and tucked it away for safekeeping. Somewhere out in California, Elizabeth's children and grandchildren might be gathered around their own Christmas tree, thinking of Elizabeth fondly just as Sylvia was. Or perhaps Elizabeth was present among them, watching over her family from a favorite spot near the fireplace, the Chimneys and Cornerstones quilt on her lap. Wherever she was, she was also with Sylvia in Elm Creek Manor, for as the Christmas Quilt had shown Sylvia that day, those she loved lived on in their handiwork and in the hearts of those who remembered them.

Tomorrow, Sylvia decided, she would string popcorn and cranberries into garlands and decorate a tree near the creek. The wildlife of Elm Creek Manor had gone too long without a Christmas feast of their own. She would search through Claudia's old papers and see if she could find the letter Elizabeth had promised to send, and perhaps with it, an address, a promising lead to the descendants she might have left behind.

But that was for tomorrow. Tonight, in the last few hours of Christmas Day, Sylvia intended to work on the Christmas Quilt, to complete a task too long neglected. In her home full of memories, she felt the presence of all those whom she loved, blessing her and wishing her well. At last she understood the true lesson of the Christmas Quilt, that a family was an act of creation, the piecing together of disparate fragments into one cloth — often harmonious, occasionally clashing and discordant, but sometimes unexpectedly beautiful and strong. Without contrast there was no pattern, as Great-Aunt Lucinda had taught her long ago, and each piece, whether finest silk or faded cotton, would endure if sewn fast to the others with strong seams — bonds of love and loyalty, tradition and faith.